NEVER TO QUIT

Never Quit!
Bob Armistead
3/96

BOB ARMISTEAD

Edited by Johnny Taeght

Front cover painting:
David Wright

Design, typography and production:
JM Productions, Inc., Brentwood, Tennessee

Front cover photography:
Dan Loftin, X-Press Studio, Nashville, Tennessee

Text production manager:
Linda Barnett

Publicity:
Schnitzer Marketing Group, Nashville, Tennessee

ISBN: 0-9635026-1-1

Library of Congress Catalog Card Number:

Eggman Publishing
2908 Poston Avenue, Suite 201
Nashville, Tennessee 37203

Table of Contents

Chapter 1
Antietam/Death's Door

Like two mighty titans of mythology, the principal armies of the North and the South had collided at Antietam Creek in Sharpsburg, Maryland. The result dazzled the world with its awesome toll of flesh and blood. Included in the overwhelming destruction was James Wilson, Jr., a twenty-year-old Confederate soldier, from Franklin, Tennessee. Franklin was a small town of about two thousand people which was situated nearly twenty miles south of the state capital in Nashville. When James awakened, he was surprised to find that he was alive. He felt his fear alone was enough to have killed him. All around was consuming quiet, an eerie calm, just like he imagined it was in heaven. The silence was so overwhelming that he couldn't even hear his own breathing. The deafening din of the previous day, which James had thought was louder than the universe could withstand, had turned into a mysterious stillness. He wondered if perhaps he was in heaven, but just didn't know it. He was so damned confused.

One thing he knew for sure was that after a battle, there were always many wounded to attend to. James sure as hell had been in a major fight. He wondered where all the wounded were. He knew the difference between a big killing and a little fight where nobody hung around to help friend or foe because both sides were on the move.

It slowly crept into his mind that the reason he wanted to hear voices was that he was unable to move to a position which would allow him to see anyone. He was numb all over, unable to move even a finger. Beaten, he lay there listening for noises

1

that might mean life. He wondered what had happened to him.

He remembered General Hood passing along the line offering encouragement as they pressed toward the church building. He recalled that Stonewall Jackson was in a pinch, for once, so Hood's beat up brigade was coming hard. It was ironic to be asked to save Jackson's ass, what with his reputation and all. It could be they were all cooked. A full 30,000 Yanks were hitting Jackson's front. The depleted ranks commanded by Hood were all that remained. If James and company, around 2,500 hard fighters from Tennessee, Texas, and Arkansas, could not hold, the dance would certainly be over.

James remembered the sick feeling he had when they fell into line, already under heavy fire. His stomach filled his throat to the point of strangulation. He had to vomit to enable himself to breathe. That had not happened to him in prior visits to the firing line. He had worried that he might be getting soft, a condition which could prove fatal.

As his dreams receded and James returned to a semi-conscious condition, he thought of the church. Of all the fights in which he had participated, he had never found anything significant or particularly strategic about the specific place of the conflict. Antietam Creek seemed the same to him. There had been thousands of men fighting and dying for that church building for reasons that were incomprehensible to him.

As he continued to drift in and out, James relived the whole ordeal. Looking beyond the colors of the 13th Virginia, he saw Yanks swarming all over that damn sunken road. There was more blue than James had ever seen. He saw one Yankee in particular very clearly. This Yank looked older than most, yet his face revealed great strength. His eyes mirrored the terrified emotions which were shared by James. Either might give or receive terror. James prevailed and took the top off of the man's head. By the time the Yank hit the ground, the look of terror had changed to one of peace.

James was the best shot in the 20th Tennessee Regiment and that meant the whole of Hood's brigade, as the 20th won the shooting contest every month. Unlike most of his battlemates, he did not have to be constantly reminded by the officers to fire low, for he always hit his target. When he looked down that slope and set his sights on that battleworn Yankee face, he knew it was over for at least one of the enemy. There sure as hell were many, many others that just kept on coming.

The Colonel of the Twentieth, Sterling Todd, was as nervous as his charges. He had seen his regiment almost cut in half since marching out of Middle Tennessee back in June of 1861. Few of them had expected the war to last through September of that year, and no one anticipated it would extend into the next year. By the time of Antietam, there were only three hundred remaining to form in front of the Dunker Church and all those damn Yankees.

From his paralyzed position, James could see the church and sunken road before him. There were dead bodies all over the building grounds and road. Yet, no movement. He wondered why no one was there to pick them up. Both sides must have pulled out. Based on what James had seen on his way to the front, he could not imagine that Marse Robert had won this one. The Army of Northern Virginia must have been headed home in defeat.

Suddenly, he began to regain reality. The uniform covering his stomach and right leg was completely bloodsoaked. The all encompassing numbness of the previous few moments was gone, replaced by shearing pain. James was no doctor, but he had seen enough wounded to know that without proper medical attention, shock could prove as deadly as a wound. Considering the amount of blood that had flowed from his body, James deduced that he must already be in a state of shock. He realized he had to tend to his wounds if he could.

He tried to raise himself, but he was just too weak and fell backward, almost passing out. As he lay there trembling from fright and shock, he hoped that someone might have seen him move. Surely some other poor bastard who had been shot to hell and back would be able to send help in his direction. No noise resounded. No talking or groaning. Not even the sound of the wind or birds. Stretcher crews should have been somewhere picking up the unfortunates, who like himself, would probably lose a limb because of the inadequate medicines or treatment. He wondered where the hell they were.

After lying motionless for quite some time, James somehow found the renewed strength from within to force himself to try to move again. The pain was still there, even more intense for the numbness had subsided. His head was clearer. Suddenly he remembered what had happened. The damn explosion had been right in front of him. Propping himself up on his left elbow, James viewed for the first time what the explosion had done to his body.

His right boot was gone, to who-knew-where along with the fourth and fifth toes of that foot. His leg bone right below his knee was exposed and above the joint, his thigh had been ripped open by shrapnel, leaving several pieces still lodged within it. His stomach was open from his right side to his navel and his clothing was sprinkled with blood. His examination of his condition forced him to become nauseous, as he collapsed and began to heave. Since James had not eaten in the last two days, his stomach was only able to regurgitate blood.

James couldn't imagine living through pain that intense. Even so, he didn't make a sound. If he was going to go, he decided he would go quietly. Taking a deep breath, he accepted his fate. Stretching out a miraculously unwounded right arm, he touched something that made him instinctively jerk away. He rolled his head over and saw Colonel Todd. As he examined him in more detail, he noticed that the Colonel's corpse included only his torso. The Colonel must have been killed by the same artillery fire that would soon kill James.

He then noticed the remains of his childhood friends, Billy Carter and John Stewart. The two had grown up with James. Billy, John, and James were best friends almost since birth, for they had all been born in the same year, in July, August, and September of 1842. Now all three seemed destined to die at the same time and place. A bitterness covered James as completely as the rolled up blanket that had been blown off his shoulder.

Seeing John and Billy made James cry. The three had been the most eligible beaus of the county before they left for war. All the girls had chased the "bandits" as the three were known to everyone in Franklin. They looked the part. James was the smallest at six feet one inch tall, weighing one hundred ninety pounds. The other two were both six feet two inches in height weighing well over two hundred ten pounds apiece. Billy was really overweight at two hundred thirty-five pounds.

They were all athletic. No one in the county was as fast as James. Once, he had beaten a horse, an old horse, in an "extra" race at the fair. It was called "extra" because it was extra short. The horse had hardly started before James was across the thirty yard course. Billy, with all his weight, was strong enough to lift a rock that weighed well over 200 pounds in a lifting contest at the County Fair.

Young John Stewart was really the luckiest of the three or so it had seemed until Antietam. He was stronger than James and faster than Billy, and he was smart. Not that James and Billy were dumb, but John was smart enough to have been invited to attend Nashville University, a college that almost everyone from Franklin who ever went to college attended. He could figure anything mathematical in his head and could memorize any piece of writing no matter how long with just one reading. He ended up being Colonel Todd's top orderly.

The three boys had wanted to join the cavalry when the fighting started. A Wilson family friend, Nathan Bedford Forrest, had been raising a cavalry outfit to operate in the state, keeping the trio, so they thought, close to home. But James' father had told them that the infantry had a stronger need than the cavalry. Accordingly, the boys hustled on down and joined the foot soldiers and marched off to fight for "southern independence."

The war had not turned out like they thought it would. The real war had made men out of boys very quickly. When survival is on the line, the maturation process accelerates. The Twentieth had been engaged in hand to hand combat all too often. At Shiloh, seventy five had been killed in one wild rush up to and, for some, into the "hornet's nest." No other outfit had any men to break through any part of that line, although a full twenty-two regiments had tried to crack it at one time or another during the day. James could not even guess how many must have died at Antietam. Lifeless, bloody bodies covered the terrain as far as his limited motion would allow him to see. The road which sank over five feet into the terrain was filled to its edge with dead from both the North and the South.The regiment had been completely overwhelmed, and most probably was wiped out.

James suddenly felt a hot, intense pain at the top of his head which caused him to black out again.

When he awakened, he put his hand to his head. He found, as he feared he might, more blood. This was a result of a deep gaping gash. The wound started at the middle of his forehead, ran directly above his right eyebrow and cut sharply toward the back before stopping at the end of his ear. The flow of blood was directly into James' right eye. Turning his head to let a stream of blood run by his eye rather than into it, he noticed for the first time that the only movement in the entire area was his. Everyone on that field, as far as he could see, was dead with the exception of him.

After contemplating the severity of his wounds, James realized why he had not received any attention. When the stretcher bearers had been there, he had been unconscious and most likely mistaken for dead. The thought lowered his spirits even further and he sank closer to the ground and began trembling. He didn't know why he was so cold for it was only September. He was freezing, he thought, probably to the point of death. At that point, his newly acquired soldier attitude began to assert itself. He calmed down quickly, pondered his death, and wondered how would it come. The options were trifold: starve, freeze or bleed. It puzzled him as to what was keeping him alive.

The sun had been shining for quite some time, and its effect parched the throat of the fallen Confederate and began to bloat the bloody bodies which carpeted the battlefield. His lips were as dry and blistered as his feet usually were after one of the many marches which Hood's veterans had endured as part of Stonewall's famous "foot cavalry." He needed water, and soon. The river was out of the question. It would be impossible for him to get there in his present state. Even if he could, the water was surely contaminated from rotting blood and human excrement. He remembered that Billy always kept a full canteen. Getting to Billy was as impossible as getting to the river. Out of desperation, he tried to yell, but nothing came out. He was too beat up to help himself at all. He had begun to drift away from consciousness when he thought that he heard footsteps approaching.

The next light that James saw was fire. Actually two fires, one on each side of him. With the exception of their light the night was dark and seemed hellious. He was wrapped in blankets. He had heard footsteps. He looked around but couldn't see anything. Something pushed up against his left foot. He then noticed the unfamiliar face of a sleeping woman nestled at his feet. He was only able to get a glimpse of her as he was too weak to raise himself for long. Still, it was enough movement to wake her.

"Don't try to move," she blurted hurriedly. "You're in shock and you've lost lots of blood. Can you understand me?" She smiled as she asked and her gaze pierced the soul of the young Confederate.

James pain was not abating and he could not force any noise from his mouth though he tried to respond. He realized he was warm and he could tell by his smell that he had been thoroughly cleaned. He was too confused to be scared and too weak to answer. It showed in his face.

"I didn't mean to get upset just then, I'm sorry," the young lady offered as she poured water over his lips. "We've stopped the bleeding and patched you up as best we could, but your leg bone is still exposed. My father will set your leg tomorrow morning before we take you back to our home in Frederick. He's gone there now and will be returning soon with a wagon."

James remembered Frederick, Maryland. The army had passed through there two days and ten miles back. It was Yankee territory. That didn't seem to matter now. The rest of the night, James floated between sleep and the semi-conscious state of calm created by the trauma to his body and the lack of immediate medical attention.

The next morning a sullen looking man about the age of James' father arrived. He seemed very sad and didn't have much to say. He approached tending to James in a matter of fact manner, similar to the way a man performed daily chores. The whole damn situation seemed strange to James. He couldn't figure why they were helping him in the first place. They treated him very well, but without compassion. Even so, their care was far better than he might have treated them and a great deal better than his friends had treated him. His friends had left him for dead while these people from Yankeeland had come to his aid. His confusion grew. However, after a liberal dose of strong home-brew whiskey which he was given so that his leg could be set, he wasn't sure of anything. The alcoholic anaesthesia coupled with the pain put him out again.

James was fortunate during the trip to Frederick for he was unconscious during most of the really rough sections of road. When he was conscious, his eyes were glazed over and their natural color, hazel, became all white. Once, the woman turned to check on him and discovered that he was awake. She looked for just a moment and quickly turned to her father and said, "I think he'll live, Poppy. He seems to be a fighter."

Although he was not capable of speech, James learned about his rescuers by listening to their conversation. The old man's surname was Johnson and the woman was his daughter, Camille. They had been at Antietam because Mr. Johnson's son served in General Hooker's Corps of the Union Army. Reports had reached the Johnsons that the young man had been wounded. Unfortunately, upon arriving at Antietam they found him, dead. During their conversations, they never called the late family member by his name. How ironic that these people were saving James after finding their own blood kin, dead, exactly opposite the point where the 20th had made its stand. And damn if that stand of Hood's hadn't saved the day after all. The Johnsons revealed that Lee had retreated south, which was a reversal, but, McClellan had been stung too badly to apply enough pressure on the retreating columns to finish them off.

Poppy Johnson was a short, five foot six inch man who carried no extra meat on his frame. His hair was grey and long. His tanned skin made James think that Johnson was a farmer by trade. Camille was blond, and boasted beautiful blue eyes. Her skin was milk white, and she seemed young, probably in her late teens.

James had no idea of the Johnson's intentions as far as it concerned him. What ever they planned, he couldn't do anything about it anyway. Yet for some reason that James could not quite logically explain, he felt secure with these people.

When the Confederate Army began its Northern thrust, expectations had been high. It was hoped that Maryland would yield recruits, provisions, and political gains in addition to a victory on Northern soil which, possibly, might put an end to the fighting. In fact, with the exception of securing provisions of all types from various Yankee posts along the way, the exact opposite had occurred. Most of the people of the state had viewed the Confederates as invaders, rather than liberators. After the cool reception the Army of Northern Virginia had received upon entering the state, James was certainly surprised by the Johnson's attitude toward him.

Only hours after arriving at the Johnson home, James slipped into a coma. His wounds, loss of blood, and lack of food, added to the exertions of the last day, were more than his system could withstand. Although shallow, his breathing continued. The Johnsons thought they were going to lose him several times but he hung on. They continued to check his leg, clean him, and keep him warm and as comfortable as they could. James had no idea he was knocking on death's front door. His mind freed him from misery.

It took him back home to Billy Carter and John Stewart. During their childhood, they would occasionally meet at a predetermined spot on the Harpeth River, which was really no more than a large creek that flowed through Williamson County. They would follow the stream up river, toward Murfreesboro, to the property of one of John's relatives. The house sat on a ridge right above the stream where the water was a wild torrent for about one hundred yards. At the end of the churning water, they had strung a thick rope all the way across, probably fifty yards, tied from tree trunk to tree trunk. About a hundred yards upstream, there was another rope tied to the biggest overhanging branch of an enormous oak tree that seemed larger than life and grew out of the side of the bank reaching almost to the center of the stream.

The three had learned early on how to shimmy up that tree from which they could use the rope to propel themselves some distance in the air before hitting the current. If they happened to get caught in the swift water, they only had to grab the rope stretched from bank to bank to be rescued and repeat the adventure. Occasionally, some of the slaves would follow the boys and jump in with them. They were welcome playmates. No one enjoyed the excursion often though as James' father had a bad attitude toward "slackers".

As far as James and his father were concerned, the slaves were no different from family and were treated as such. No one on the farm, even James, was ever beaten, even if punishment was warranted. The slaves came and went on the farm as they pleased without supervision for there was total trust among all the Wilsons. James remembered when one of their favorite slaves, Uncle Silas, died. The Wilsons had been just as upset as if one of their own blood relatives had passed away. Old Silas and his wife, Jessie Mai, had practically raised Mr. Wilson and James.

Mai was a great cook. Her skills incited the whole family, black and white to perform great work. All of the slaves on the Wilson farm were offspring of Old Silas and Mai. Being as close as he was to his slaves, Mr. Wilson never allowed any of his people to be sold away. The tremendous productivity of the Wilson place attracted buyers for both human as well as agricultural commodities.

The farm was eighteen hundred acres of pure beauty surrounded by rolling hills that formed the beginnings of the great Smokey Mountains in East Tennessee. The main house was located about three miles south of the town square and almost one half mile from the Carter home which was the last house within the city limits. Around the two story red brick and clapboard structure were the various buildings associated with the proper operation of a large, profitable plantation. Two privies, a barn for horses, three implement sheds, and a chicken coup were all clean and whitewashed to the point of looking painted. In contrast, the main house with its dark red bricks, stood out enough to be seen a mile or better south on one of the near ridges. The adjacent yard was immaculately groomed and the fences also were whitewashed, adding even more to the meticulous appearance of the house.

The entire workload of the farm was accomplished with only ten field hands in addition to James and his father. Many people wondered how Jim Wilson made as much as he did out of his place. His formula for success followed a very basic premise. Everybody worked and worked hard. Every person was capable of performing every job on the farm, and all did, including the Wilsons.

Jim Wilson was not an outwardly religious man and didn't use the Bible for every decision he made. But, he knew the difference between right and wrong. In 1855, he gathered everyone together and they all sensed something big was coming.

"From this day forward, everyone on this place is free. You can go wherever you want whenever you want."

A smile creased the face of Joshua, who was named from the Bible and was the son of Uncle Silas. Others even laughed out loud. They had always been free to do as they pleased. Mr. Wilson was just making it "fissol."

He continued on with his announcement, the content of which was most unexpected.

"I have been saving some part of all the hard money the farm has taken in for your care. Now you can have your share and move on if you want to," he offered. "Here's your papers."

Most nodded and mumbled to one another. Some even took the papers to read. All of the Negroes on the Wilson place had been taught to read, write, and do a few numbers even though it was illegal in the Southern states. After perusing the documents, several uttered thanks. Then as a unit, they departed and returned to the work which was the one thing they all understood.

Being only 13 years into this life, James couldn't comprehend his father's concerns and actions. He failed to see the importance of telling free people they were free people when they had known it all long.

"I don't see why you're so worried, anyway. There ain't nobody leaving our place. They love us as much as we love them, and the Northerners won't be able to take people away, will they?" he asked of his father, whose great insight had allowed him to see the clouds of war gathering for some time.

When the news spread about the freeing en masse of the Wilson people, the plantation soon became the focal point of all slave traders headed in any direction. One buyer who came from just east of Memphis was Bedford Forrest. Forrest, like Jim Wilson, believed that it was just a matter of time until commerce based on slave labor would cease. He wanted to see the effect on the farm of such a radical measure as total and legal freedom. It was as he had expected. Only two of the former slaves left the farm and they headed north. The rest remained and helped the farm become dramatically more productive.

Jim Wilson and Forrest rapidly developed a deep friendship. Forrest was a big, broad shouldered man standing six feet, three inches tall, and was a straight talker, a trait which seemed odd for a trader. He remained on the Wilson farm for several weeks and worked two other land deals in Nashville while learning Wilson's techniques in running a farm.

The Wilsons, like almost everyone who ever came in contact with the man, found Nathan Bedford Forrest to be totally self made and motivated. Raised in the wilderness of Tennessee, in the Chapel Hill area, Forrest had grown up in poverty. He was the oldest of ten children of a rural blacksmith who had died when Bedford was only sixteen years old. His father's death left the teenager in charge of the family's welfare. It was a responsibility he would latch onto.

Until that time in Forrest's life, his education in books had been sparse, but his experiences in life were bountiful. As a youth, he had once tracked a panther which had attacked his mother, as she carried a basket of chickens. He followed the big cat for three days. Scarred and bruised from the ordeal, young Forrest finally treed the cat, waited till first light, then summarily killed and scalped the beast as retribution for the near fatal attack upon his mother. As a provider, he was most sufficient. Through diligence and the application of God-given-common sense, Forrest was able to greatly improve his family's station in life.

Persistence and a deep understanding of life's requirements for survival in a harsh time and place, held young Bedford in good stead. He was son, brother, father, and teacher all in one for his family. Like so many from the back country, he became adept at trading. In the beginning, he bartered foodstuffs and cotton for household needs and a few coins. Eventually he traded in livestock. He soon realized, however, that horse trading and selling farm produce had its limitations. His goal was to insure that his family did more than avoid poverty. He wanted them to prosper.

In the early 1850's Forrest concluded that cotton and the slaves with which to work it were the only avenue to financial security. In 1851, he became licensed as a broker in Memphis to trade real estate and slaves. Then began the period of Forrest's life in which he amassed great monetary wealth which brought with it social acceptance. Both his slave trade and real estate businesses grew to the point that he soon controlled thousands of plantation acres in Northern Mississippi while becoming the most respected slave trader in the area. As the decade of the 1850's neared its end, Forrest's wealth approached one million dollars.

At the same time, sectional tensions were increasing and war was becoming more imminent with each passing day. Forseeing that in one way or another slavery would eventually end, Forrest quit the slave trading business in order to concentrate his energies on cotton production at his plantations. When war came he enlisted as a private in a regiment of cavalry being raised in Memphis. He would remain an enlisted man for a very short period of time.

Chapter 2
Recovery/Love

James' coma had progressed into a semi-conscious dream-like state when he looked up at that black face and called Joshua's name.

"Y' mus be de dumess moze vile pusson I eva laid my eyes on," replied Richard, the Johnson's black foreman.

He had listened to James cursing in his unconsciousness for the last six days. James had not had much real education to speak of beyond some ability to read, write, and a little arithmatic. His most recent education had been as to the ways of war. That lifestyle dominated his dreams.

"Miss Camille has set y' leg an pached d' res as bes she could. Youse bin out fo nilly six days. Dey really thot dey would be a diggin a grave out hind d' pen, not eben nowing what name t' put on d' marka," Richard went on.

James had to chuckle at the remark, a chuckle which caused a sharp pain to remind him of his wounds. For some reason, he never understood, from the time he saw that black face, he knew he was going to live. Immediately, Richard summoned Poppy and Camille into the room. It took all of his strength, but James was able to explain to them who he was and where he had come from. With those words this dying Rebel was transformed into a wounded young man in the eyes of his saviours. As his strength ebbed, Camille gently touched his hand.

"Don't try to speak anymore, it will take too much effort. You need to rest. You're in our hands now," she said assuredly.

There was a genuine sense of caring in her voice. James lay there, thinking of Franklin and his father and friends at home as the Johnsons discussed his future care. Even in his present condition, James longed to get back to Franklin as quickly as possible. He realized he would have to be patient and wait, even though patience was not one of his greatest virtues. Franklin would prove a long trip and at this point, even the act of sitting up in bed had to be a nearly impossible challenge.

About an hour later, Camille returned with food. For a while, as she fed him chicken broth with bread crumbs, she didn't speak a word, and used only eye contact for communication. Even then she constantly avoided his gaze. When she finally spoke, it was only about the food or the treatment or progress of his wounds. Her words and her deeds were delivered very softly.

James was unaware of it but even while he was out, they had managed to get some food into him. During his comaic exile, Camille had listened to James' ramblings and had heard more than enough to embarrass her into a quiet shyness. He wanted desperately to communicate his gratefulness, and did the best he was able to do which was to raise his right hand, with which he touched her knee as she bent toward him to administer the healing broth. The movement startled her so much that Camille loosened her grip on the soup bowl, spilling its hot contents all over James' chest.

The embarrassed belle rushed around the room trying to find something to remove the soup. Seeing that she could find nothing to help her in this predicament, she slowly sank into the chair next to the bed and began to cry. The combination of the war at her doorsteps and the loss of her own brother in the bitter struggle had finally taken its toll. The pain from the soup could not compare with the hurt of which James had become accustomed. He took her hand in his and held it until she looked at him. With as much strength as he could muster, he smiled and uttered the word, "no." Then he drifted off to sleep.

He was awakened by a familiar and unmistakable sound. A sound James had heard all too often the last several months. It was the result of an officer's sabre scabbard slapping against his leather belt. His insecurities led him to believe that for some reason the Johnsons had called on the nearest Yankee authorities in order to transfer him to much drearier and cramped quarters. He had heard horror stories about Yankee prisons.

"Don't move or make a sound," Mr. Johnson whispered as he hurried into the room.

Richard was close on his heels receiving orders to meet the cavalryman and get him on his way as quickly as possible. Poppy was very explicit in his instructions.

"Don't give anything away about our guest or we'll all get hauled off to jail," he warned.

In the last few days, James had been able to eat fairly substantial food, so some strength had returned to his skeletal body. He was prepared to move as quickly as he had to even though he could tell that there was no way Mr. Johnson was going to let him be taken. It was the first opportunity for them to really talk, and there was a hell of a lot for both to find out.

"I used to live in Georgia," Poppy recalled. "We moved here in the mid-fifties. Camille was just a young girl then. She didn't have a chance to know the South the way I did."

James found that Poppy, whose real name was Reuben, knew the Middle Tennessee area very well and had even visited Franklin on several occasions in his youth. He spoke fondly of the slow and graceful life which he had known in his past. When he had made the move North, he had brought Richard with him. Although Maryland had always been a slave state, Richard was free and earned an honest wage. Like Jim Wilson, Reuben Johnson had freed all his slaves early on, but Richard was the only one who stayed with him. The rest were too intimidated. James found that even though they were on different sides of the fight, they shared a feeling they would always have in common. That feeling was compassion. After hearing Poppy's words, James knew there was no way these Yankees would ever turn him over to the provost.

The venturesome cavalryman had stopped merely for food and water and never suspected that the enemy was in his midst.

After receiving an ample supply of provisions including some homemade apple brandy, he moved on in search of the Federal Army. It was his men whom he sought, not the enemy.

James was awake most of that night thinking about the war and wondering if he belonged in the middle of the whole damn thing. He had paid a tremendously high price for what he believed and had every right to walk, or in his case limp away from the fighting right then and there and not be criticized. As his mental debate continued, he knew that he was never to quit. He vowed he would return to the battlefield. Not for slavery, for he knew in his heart and soul that no man had the right to own another. He would return because it was his right to decide where and how he was to live. The possibility that their homes might be violated was the reason most of the Southerners had entered the war. James shared their fear and their conviction to keep Northerners in the North.

Another thought that kept him awake was concern about what was happening at home since the young men who were the strength of the South had enlisted and subsequently left for war. Since early in 1862, the Union Army had been in control of most of Tennessee. Included in the occupation was Nashville and the surrounding area where he presumed his father to be living. God only knew what acts of horror those blue bastards might take toward people like James' father. He wondered if his house was still standing for it had been over a year since he had received any letters or communications of any type from home.

Weeks passed as Camille continued to feed and care for James. One December morning she served news with breakfast.

"Ambrose Burnside has been put at the head of the Army of the Potomac," she said very excitedly. "We are moving on Richmond, even now.

"So as soon as you can help yourself, you can leave freely with no more war to fight. Surely, Burnside will end this thing quickly!"

In her glee, Camille had forgotten from whence this underweight convalescent had come. Her words stung him as badly as had the Yankee shrapnel.

During their time together, James and Camille had become very close, and he had learned how to temper his own patriotic enthusiasm when they talked. The temperance took a great deal of concentrated effort, but he did not want to say anything to hurt her as she had worked so hard to heal him. He really couldn't understand how she could delight in something that she should have known would cause him great anguish. It seemed to contradict the months she had labored to rid him of his pain.

"I know Burnside is a fighter. But, so is Bobby Lee. Burnside will be the third such general to butt heads with Lee, and I bet a dollar Confederate to a dime Federal that the Yanks come out with a bloody nose again," he predicted. "And they'll be darned lucky if that's all that's bleeding."

James sounded most confident describing General Lee as the master of the science of war but he was wasn't exactly elated with the new Northern commander for Burnside's aggressive reputation was well known and he possessed a seemingly countless number of men in his command. James recalled that it had been Burnside's Corps that hit that damn, little unworthy bridge at Antietam. As a matter of fact, it was known as "Burnsides Bridge" from that day forward.

By the time James was able to sit up on his own, news had reached the Johnsons that Fredericksburg had been virtually destroyed. If Camille's attitude was any indication, the Army of Northern Virginia would be next in line to feel the sting. With each passing day, James grew more and more nervous until he thought his heart might pound out of his chest. He was nervous over the war and had noted some strange feelings he was starting to harbor for Camille. Thoughts of her seemed always present in his tormented brain.

Besides her, all he could think about was getting up and out. And he tried, too. Through trial and error, mostly error, he discovered that he was not going anywhere without help. All he could do was wait and hope his wounds mended quickly.

His mind often wandered to better days and he thought of his old regiment. He wondered if the Twentieth was still a unit and who might be leading it. James greatly missed his friends from within the ranks, most of whom he knew were probably in a different and better place than he. Death seemed a better condition than survival in many cases. For those who had survived, he prayed knowing that another big fight was coming and that many more would not live through it. Each death ended the life of a soldier and began the life of a widow or childless mother.

Before Christmas news came that Burnside had blundered badly. With Lee firmly entrenched on the heights overlooking Fredericksburg with 65,000 war hardened veterans, the Yanks had bravely, yet stupidly, advanced up those slopes into the most concentrated and effective fire the war had seen to date. Whole divisions of the Union Army had been obliterated and several corps were cut up badly. Lee's legions had suffered only small casualties while inflicting tremendous damage. Once again, Richmond was saved and the boys in blue were skedaddling north.

"God bless R.E. Lee," James prayed.

Since the time his hide had been saved, he had become very close to these transplanted Rebs. James found it increasingly difficult to outwardly show his true feelings of joy in the presence of the Johnsons. The war had brought with it an array of new emotions and feelings to its participators. James was feeling things that he had never felt before even in war. These emotional feelings were so intense that they seemed physical. He hadn't said a word to anyone, especially Camille, but there was a queasy feeling that grabbed his gut every time she touched him, an occurrence which took place at least every other day, for that was how often his bandages had to be changed.

Just like Billy Carter and John Stewart and all the other young bucks at home, James had at one time or another ventured to Nashville and laid down a silver dollar for the only real sex any of them had ever experienced. That is other than the Jenkins twins, Molly or Missy, who had always been available for a roll in the hay when no money was available. Those situations, however, were purely physical and lasted only a fleeting moment. The Jenkins twins, well, they weren't really much to look at.

The fact that James had never had any kind of relationship, to speak of, with a woman made his new feelings very difficult to deal with. Confused and baffled, he wished someone were there to help him sort it all out. Unfortunately, his help was a thousand miles away wondering whether or not he still had a namesake.

By the beginning of 1863, James had become adept at bed bathing himself; therefore, Camille wasn't as close as often as before. When she was near, he felt he would go out of his mind. Each time he felt the gaze of those cool blue eyes, he wanted to hide so as not to show his passion. He was too modest to realize it, but his eyes were causing romantic palpatations within the heart of Camille.

Back home, none of the girls he had known had blond hair like hers. Its unique quality seemed to make her eyes stand out like the moon on top of Winstead Hill. That was the peaceful hill which formed the boundary of his family's place and the property of the Smithson's. Earlier in his life, he had admired that moon every night unless it was shrouded by clouds. That shroud added to the mystique similarly to the way Camille's hair often fell over her eyes, allowing only traces of their beauty to be seen.

Winstead Hill reminded James of the Smithsons, a thought which quickly brought Shiloh into his memory. The Smithsons had lost their only two children at Shiloh on the second day of the battle. He pondered as to how they could get along without the hope of their sons return. He knew that his father was helping his neighbors as much as he could, if in fact he could. Reality then invaded to remind him that he didn't know where or how his own father was faring.

Maryland's cold January weather kept Camille indoors more than before. Most of that time was spent at bedside of the fallen warrior where they read newspapers and talked. Camille did most of the reading, James most of the talking. More often than not in an attempt to keep from saying something controversial the subject matter was something other than the war. James found those times to be very enjoyable, yet very perplexing because of the conflict between his stomach and throat. Often, he would catch himself staring so deeply at Camille, thinking about his feelings, that she would blush as if she knew his thoughts. Immediately, she would change course and begin talking about riding or the farm or life after the war.

"I have talked with Poppy, and if the war ends before you get well, that we'd, I mean, he'd like to have you stay on and help work the place," she offered as she changed his dressings.

James couldn't respond, even though her offer confirmed that she felt something too. Saying no more, she gently squeezed his hand and left the room.

That night his dinner was brought in by Richard. James asked about Camille and why she hadn't served his meal. He was told that she was resting in her room from an extra amount of work done that day. Damn, if he wasn't confused! He not only had to deal with his own feelings, but, hers as well, and without the benefit or the support of anyone else. War and women had joined to thoroughly confuse a previously well focused lad. He thought of asking for advice from Richard, but didn't for he knew the black foreman held him only in contempt.

To say that James didn't sleep that night would certainly be an understatement. He lay there thinking about all his father had told him about sex and marriage and how to love a woman. But, dammit, fighting a war somewhere in Maryland was not the setting where he supposed love would blossom. A war which would bring about the death of over six hundred-thousand Americans, had conceived love.

The next morning, when Camille returned to James with his early meal, she admitted that she had been too embarrassed to see him the previous night. She empathized with his feelings of his home and realized how much he longed to get well and head off in that direction. She also felt she had spoken too hastily concerning the war's end and especially his staying on. James stopped her before she had a chance to say more.

"It really doesn't matter much now anyway," he said. "It's obvious that I can't go anywhere anytime soon. It's been right at three months and I can barely get out of bed. Besides that, even with Burnsides' defeat, which could mean another Southern thrust into the North, I doubt that our boys would head for the same general area.

"So, I don't expect to see any boys in grey ambling through this neck of the woods to snatch me up and take me home. Like it or not, I'm here for awhile," he explained; then added, "And I'm beginning to like it."

At that they both smiled and looked into each other's eyes for what seemed like an eternity. Then Camille rose, and without speaking a word, left the room. He realized then that it was not his stomach that had been causing his throat all those problems. It was his heart.

Under Camille's watchful care, James' wounds were healing rapidly, but not fast enough to please him. He had two entirely different emotions tugging on him to get up and out. Young Wilson feared that his leg had received a permanent injury though he had not yet attempted to stand on it. With the exception of Camille's daily visits, time passed very slowly.

By the middle of January, Lincoln had followed the example set by Jim Wilson and Reuben Johnson and declared all slaves held in rebellious states or those that had declared secession, to be free. James found the proclamation a very strange doctrine. Why not free all people everywhere if he was going to free any?

Joe Hooker had succeeded Burnside as the head of the Eastern Yanks and Bragg had won a draw at Murfreesboro, Tennessee, very near Franklin. That was just too damn close to home for comfort. James ached for wanting to know what was happening at home and the condition of his father. Even compared to his new found feelings for Camille, his father remained the most important person in his life.

James' mother, Clarre, had died when he was born. He had never really known the cause of her death other than that childbirth was just too much for her. His father had always shown James the love for two. The only family he had ever known was his father, and it sure as hell worried James not knowing how he was.

On his Tennessee farm, Jim Wilson, emoted the same feelings. He had not heard from his son even though James had written often prior to Antietam. The wartime postal service had its flaws. He, of course, didn't know where his son was, or if he was even alive. He had written to the Confederate government in Richmond on several occasions inquiring about his son, but never received a reply to his inquiries.

In his heart, James knew that his father was not dead. The older Wilson was too smart for that. He would sacrifice every worldly possession he owned before endangering his life or the lives of his people. He had built a small fortune once and that ability would always be with him. James figured that if things were really hot in the middle Tennessee area, his father was probably not at home, or even in the state for that matter.

With the arrival of February, the patient's healing began to progress more quickly and he found that, with help, he was able to stand for very brief periods. In addition to the weight he had lost as an infantryman on the move receiving very scant rations, he had lost more during the initial stages of his downtime. He weighed barely 150 pounds. If he stood too long, it caused him to become pale and very nauseous.

Camille was always there to steady him. Her touch alone was enough to give him strength to continue trying. His six foot one inch frame which had once easily carried 200 pounds and more had begun to look like a dying tree whose branches had given up the fight. His feelings for Camille were becoming obvious as she noted the way the muscles in his arm and back jumped with excitement at her touch. Slowly, the time spent standing increased until James gained enough strength to sit in a large wing chair to take his meals. He felt as if he was a damned burden in his weakened condition so he began to eat more and more in an effort to regain his lost weight and strength.

It amazed him how his feelings had changed since beginning the Northward invasion. He began to feel guilt about his past attitudes. He came to understand that the Johnsons were just like him. They too hated the war and the very reasons that brought it on. It was the rich extremists, on both sides, who were at its origins. Still something inside continually chided James that he had to go back as quickly as he could. Why couldn't his head and heart agree? The mental strain was worse than his wounds. Physically, at least, he was getting better.

From time to time when no one was around, James would attempt to stand and take a step or two, using a chair or another piece of furniture in the room as support. He usually waited until the middle of the day when everyone was out of the house doing chores before falling about his attic room in an attempt to relearn how to walk. Progress was painfully slow and after the months he had spent on his back, he knew there would be very little that he could do to repay the Johnsons. He also feared that he would be able to contribute very little to the Twentieth and the war effort. The only way he could be of any help to his friends, North or South, would be strapped to the back of a horse. With his walking the way it was, he wasn't even sure he would be able to sit in a saddle.

From the daily aromas that drifted up from below, he had reasoned that the kitchen was right below his window. One day right after lunch, he decided he would try to make it to the kitchen to test his strength. Although he had almost no use of his right leg, his left leg and his arms were strong enough to support him to make the trip down and back up if he didn't stumble along the way. He had to stop for several minutes on three different occasions along the way in order to catch his breath and rest. He was very quiet and reached the kitchen in less than forty minutes. Upon his arrival, he realized something he should have expected. His test could go no further until he could go it alone, unsupported, for there was no fencing or anything else for help between the house and the barn.

He would have to be able to walk that trip by himself before he could ever consider heading South. It took him at least twice as long to get back to his bed and the exertion involved so thoroughly "wipt" him that he was still sleeping when Camille came with his dinner. Something in her look or the questioning manner in which she talked made him think that she knew what he'd done, although she never mentioned it.

For the next several days he was often overly impatient with her. He knew what it was that his heart had been telling him. He just didn't know how to express his feelings, especially to Camille. James had very little experience with that particular emotion. He worried, that she somehow knew of his feelings and that scared the day-lights out of him. When Camille wasn't with him, he spent his time waiting and watching. He awaited news, any news about the war and watched "Big Red," Camille's gelding, and dreamed about riding him into Franklin.

Through secondhand Yankee papers, with their damn slanted views, he learned that the Federals had begun drafting men for their armies. He also learned of a general named Grant of Donelson fame who was falling all over himself trying to take Vicksburg, Mississippi, and read that old Burnside had been transferred to Tennessee, of all places. Joe Hooker being placed in command of the Army of the Potomac didn't bother James so much when he remembered more than once seeing the backs of Hooker's men yielding to the onslaught of Hood's hard hitting veterans from Texas and Tennessee.

With the exception of the news about Burnside, which bothered him from a personal viewpoint, James figured that the South was holding its own. That, in and of itself, was good news. As he put all the pieces of the puzzle together in his mind, he combined the tremendous victory at Fredericksburg with Vicksburg remaining open to link east and west. Due to the fact that the North had been forced to institute a draft, he surmised that war sentiment in the North was seemingly very low and he even rationalized that the South might just be winning the damn thing. He continued to work on trying to walk and even began exercising in bed by flexing and moving in ways that caused his muscles to respond and gain strength.

On April 17, James surprised the Johnsons by meeting them in the kitchen just as Camille was starting to his room with his dinner. A couple of weeks earlier, Camille had brought some of her brothers old clothes up to James' room so they would be ready when needed. The remains of the butternut uniform of which James had been so proud had been burned long before, so he was wearing one of the two alternating sleeping gowns that Poppy had made available. Even James joined in the laughter at the sight he knew he presented there leaning against the door frame.

None of the Johnsons had envisioned that the new, old clothes would be needed that soon. In a joyous mood, Richard and Poppy hustled him upstairs to try and make him presentable. They quickly found that the younger Johnson had been somewhat shorter and, heftier than James. The size difference caused a very gangly look.

"I'm glad to see you up and around, and I'm afraid I know what it means." Poppy said as his face grew solemn.

At her father's words, the blood rushed from Camille's face and she clapped her hands over her mouth and ran outside. James tried to follow but, found that mobility and any kind of agility were two things he still lacked. He would have fallen flat on his face if Poppy's strong hands had not been there to catch him. With the help of Poppy and Richard, he made his way to the front porch where he found Camille who was still crying. His eyes began to water and his throat contract as he pulled himself closer to the only woman he had ever had any genuine loving feelings for. Poppy and Richard quickly departed after depositing their burden on the steps. He wasn't sure what to say or how to begin, but somehow he did.

"You know that I love you, don't you," he could hardly believe what he was hearing himself say. "You're bound to be able to see that aren't you?"

"Yes," she whispered, so quietly that he could hardly hear her. "I feel it, too."

Weak from the physical and mental exertion, he reached out for the help he so desperately needed. Feeling her arms wrap tightly around him, James felt a tingle throughout his still healing body. He couldn't compare it to anything he had ever felt including his first taste of battle. She helped him onto the second step of the porch so that he would have a support from the higher step. Then she slid next to him.

"What can we do?" she asked, wiping the tears from her cheeks.

Without answering, he touched her lips with his fingers and slowly leaned forward to kiss her. Not hard or forcefully, but, soft, so soft, with more feeling than he had ever before known he had within him. Then he pulled away, just enough so that their foreheads were still leaning against each other and answered her question. Her taste would not be forgotten, and he looked away deep in thought.

"God only knows what's ahead for either of us. For the first time in my life, I feel things that I've only heard about. Things I supposed would never be a part of me. I don't understand why something so good has to hurt so bad."

He didn't know if he was making any sense at all with all that was running through his head and heart as he rambled on.

"I only know what I feel, right now, deep, deep down," he continued.

"I don't want you to leave me," she whispered again. "I need you. I want you more and more every day, and I know you need me too. This thing is such a mess. How could I have fallen in love with a rebel, of all people? An invader of our country?

"Before you came into our lives, there was no one who ever needed me. But, you did, from the beginning.

"You didn't need me in your heart at first, I know that. But, over the months I've seen the need grow along with your love. When I realized that you were going to recover, I almost had a breakdown. I so wanted you to live but couldn't imagine what I'd do if you did. But, I began to see a change in your eyes and touch and even talked to Poppy about you staying," she paused.

"Oh, how I've prayed for the war to end, so you wouldn't have to leave. Even with our different ideas about the war, just watching and listening to you has been a source of joy and strength to me," she continued.

"At first, I thought I was maybe replacing my brother, Tom, with you but I soon found out the truth. I don't love you like a brother. No one could ever fill the void left by Tom. My feelings for you have grown stronger and stronger all this time so that now no one could ever take your place in my heart. I have dreaded this day for months, hoping that it would never come, but I always knew that it would.

"Sometimes, I wished I would just wake up one morning and find you gone. I thought that would be such a clean break and somehow make it easier to lose you."

"I could never do that," he interrupted. "Even if I wasn't in love with you, I couldn't run out on you after you and your father saved my life with no regard for who I was. Anyway, there's not too far I could go without my nurse to help."

As she leaned her head against his left shoulder, Camille began to whimper softly. Not knowing how to comfort her with words beyond what he had already said, all James could do was hold her as closely as his trembling body would allow him.

Having been up for more than an hour, James began to feel very dizzy and suggested that she call her father for help to get him back upstairs into his bed. Neither of them knew it, but help was standing directly behind them in the doorway. Camille's father was not eavesdropping but was prepared to come to James' aid should the strain have become too great. Poppy helped them both to their feet.

"You two seem to have a problem. Even if you were not inclined to head South," he said to James, "and I understand that you are and why, it would only be a matter of time before your presence here was discovered.

"That discovery, I'm afraid, would lead to certain imprisonment," he explained. "On the other hand, the odds are rather long that the two of you could travel from here to Tennessee safely. I've already lost one child to this war and I don't believe I could stand to lose both of my children, no matter which side I'm on.

"James, you've taken a special place in my heart, too and losing you is something I don't look forward to. I reckon we should all get a good night's rest before trying to figure a way out of this mess we're in."

Poppy turned and walked into the house a few steps leaving them alone just long enough for James to hold her once again.

James felt a quiver in her body similar to the one he had felt earlier and he pressed his lips against hers with the gentleness of a soft breeze.

"God knows I need you," he said as he turned to head upstairs to his bed and much needed rest.

The next morning, more strength had returned to James' healing body. Still, he was drained emotionally. The night's rest had not been so good and there were still no clear answers to the problems at hand. His head and heart were still in conflict and would remain so as long as he needed to be home in Tennessee and to be in Maryland with Camille. He knew that on his own, if he had a horse, he could somehow make it South to his home. But not if he had company. Especially if that company was a young girl. In fact, he had no horse, money, or even the clothes he was wearing to call his own.

And what if the two of them went? What would they find when they got there? Probably, there would be nowhere to live and no means of support without help from his father. After two years of war, he didn't feel inclined to lean on anybody when it came to supporting a wife. A wife? Before that moment he had not really thought of their relationship in the matrimonial sense. If only he could talk with his father, he knew Jim Wilson would know what to do. He continued to maintain his belief that his father was alive and safe. With all the turmoil, he wondered if he could still be at home.

Knowing that he was not yet ready to travel, there was still time that could be spent with Camille in relative safety. He determined that no matter what else might happen he would spend whatever time he had left at the Johnson home as close to Camille as possible. That, for now, would be a source of pleasure. He lay there dreaming of the war being over and his two families being together in peace.

After a while, Camille arrived with his breakfast, thinking he would be too tired to come downstairs after the exertions of the night before. She certainly knew that she was exhausted. Seeing her, he knew he could wait no longer. As she set the tray beside his bed, he reached out and touched her cheek with his fingertips and felt her soft golden hair fall around the back of his arm. He began trembling with emotion.

"I want you and I don't think it can wait."

"It's all right." she answered. "My father and Richard have gone to try to find transportation to the South, hopefully, for both of us."

She leaned over him and their lips touched as his hands dropped to her slender shoulders and pulled her to him. As he pulled her dress off of her shoulders, he saw that she was wearing nothing underneath. That revelation caused a sensation to arise in him that was so hot that he began to sweat.

"I love you," she whispered, stepping out of the bunched up dress which lay on the floor.

He could not respond, but continued to caress her with his lips until he had lowered his mouth between her breasts, causing her to throw her head back and shudder with excitement.

"Hold me close," she smiled as they fell back on the bed.

James shouted, after they had been lying there silently for about an hour , "I must be going crazy, dammit! How can this be happening?"

"Don't worry," she said. "Even if you have to leave without me, I'll wait. I'll be here. Or I can always come to you later after you've had time to find out what we're up against."

"Being without you even one day will be hell." James moaned, "If I can help it, it won't come to pass."

"I know. But, Poppy thinks that there would be very little chance of us both making it to Tennessee with things being as they are," she said calmly.

"We might not even get out of the state before your accent gives us away. And you or we, would have to be in constant hiding, at least, until we crossed the Potomac. Maybe, even longer."

James didn't answer, but, she knew he knew what "the real world" was when he heard it. He had lived enough of it in the last few years.

Poppy returned late that afternoon, having achieved no success in his search. It was agreed that he would find one stout horse for James' trip home. Poppy told James that he could send money for the horse when he sent for Camille. The thought of possibly losing his daughter after having lost a son to the war, made Poppy begin to cry. Prior to leaving the company of James and Camille, he agreed that if a suitable animal could be had by April 30th, James would start his journey then.

Within a week, a horse was found for $15 Union, that could carry James, at least as far as Richmond. Camille and James went out every morning and late afternoon to practice riding and, more importantly, to be alone. The riding came much easier to James than he had thought it would as did the being alone. He used his left foot to mount anyway, so his major problem as far as horses were concerned was staying in the saddle once he got there. That was not a problem with his physical encounters with Camille. Whenever they would stop riding for any reason, they made love, always more passionately than the time before.

By the night of the twenty-ninth of the month, all the necessary arrangements had been made. Poppy extended his hand, knowing that James would be gone before they could see each other again.

"Tom's gone now, after fighting for what he believed and I don't want to lose another son. Good luck on your journey, and remember, we plan to see you again, so be very careful," Poppy warned.

James was too choked to answer, but Poppy understood, and turned to leave the two lovers together for what he thought might be the last time.

Some minutes later, unable to speak because of the gigantic lump in his throat, James took Camille by the hand in hopes of finding strength in her once again. He did.

"All the hate I ever felt because of this war is gone now. After the time I have spent here, I just don't see the use in hating anymore. As much as I want to stay, I know I have to go. I have to find my father. I really don't know yet whether I'll go back to the fight or not, but I have to find my family. No matter what, I will be with you again one day," he promised.

"I love you, James Wilson, and I'll wait as long as I have to. If you don't come to me, I'll come to you. Nothing can keep us apart forever, not war or hundreds of miles between us."

That night, there was no love making, only fanatical embracing. The next morning, as Poppy had thought, James had saddled and was prepared to leave long before day break. As he was about to mount after one long lasting embrace, Camille looked into the face of the only man she had ever loved.

Don't ever look back," she begged, "just keep on going and get through to the rebel lines." "Rebel" lines made James smile. He kissed her briefly, mounted and rode south without another word.

Chapter 3
To Richmond/Home

Camille's tailoring abilities allowed James' appearance to resemble that of a civilian. She had worked long hours adjusting her brother's old clothes, both in length and width so that they fit close to perfectly. He actually looked every bit the part of a young Maryland farmer. Because of his heavy Southern accent, he only traveled by night in order to avoid as many people as possible until he reached the Potomac River. He had decided that if he happened to be stopped and questioned, he would explain his wounds at Antietam truthfully, with but one exception, from a Northern point of view, that he had been wounded by Southern rather than Northern artillery.

Because James kept to the woods and stayed completely out of sight during daylight, he didn't know until later that the Potomac area was crawling with Yankee cavalry making their way south in advance of the new Union offensive which was mounting in order to strike at Lee. Had he been spotted and apprehended, he would have spent the rest of any fighting days behind bars if he was lucky. If not, he would have been hanged as a spy. Traveling slowly, by the light offered by the moon and stars, it took him three days to reach Virginia. They were three damn lonely days. He often thought of the Johnsons and all that they had taught him. Many times, he almost turned back and decided to fight no more, but he had to stay the course. He recalled the taste of Camille's sweet lips and the touch of her soft body and feared he might never taste or feel them again. It amazed him how a man would be willing to change for the love of a woman. His thoughts always returned to his father or why he had been in Maryland in the first place. He continuted his journey south, knowing he would either find Lee or reach Richmond. Either would suit him fine.

His fifth day in the saddle he reached the Confederate lines, finding that Jackson had surprised the hell out of Hooker on the Union right, at Chancellorsville. Initially, he encountered only the walking wounded and other noncombatants such as teamsters, or medical personnel. It seemed that Jackson's flanking movement had been a total success. Indeed, the Yanks had been completely routed from the field.

James was bone tired and mighty sore from his ride, but ached even more to find the Twentieth wherever it might be, if in fact it still existed. He was forced to face the painful realization that he would never fight with the infantry again. He would be unable to keep up. It would take some time to get used to his disabilities, even on horseback. He was damned determined to succeed.

In better times back home, he used to ride all over the county in a single day. Since James' father was much more than a crop farmer, he had counted on James early in his youth to know and to work his livestock. Pure-blooded animals always had great spirit and required a good deal of hustle on James' part when one would leave the farm having jumped some low or broken point in the split-rail fencing that bounded the Wilson property. There were also 200-300 head of cattle that required tending. Therefore, riding became second nature. Now, however, he was handicapped by the loss of two toes and by a leg wound that would never completely heal. An activity which had once been sport had become labor.

He remembered when he was fifteen and he and his father had ridden their horses to the Tennessee-Alabama border to swim in the Tennessee river. They never traveled a real road on the whole trip, coming or going. Except for coffee and corn meal, they carried no food with them, living off the land by hunting rabbit, squirrel, and deer. The trip took nearly three weeks and they were damn glad to get back home. With a roof over his head and a real bed to sleep in, James slept for thirty consecutive hours. They had great fun and James learned the ropes of living.

While the news that trickled back from the front was great in terms of Confederate successes, there were rumors of one terrible disaster for the South. Stonewall had been shot. Apparently, the incident had occurred after dark when Jackson was making a personal reconnaissance of the ground in front of his corps. Upon reentering Confederate lines, he and his party were mistaken for Yankee cavalry and fired upon by their own troops. The bluebellies themselves could not have done worse damage to the Southern cause. The reaction of the troops as the news flowed through the army was extremely dramatic. Men of all age and rank were dazed, often crying, as if victory which was overwhelmingly theirs, had been abruptly snatched away. Jackson's troops believed they won battles as a result of the leadership of their beloved commander. The effect of his loss would be immeasurable.

Eventually word began to circulate that the wound had not killed the great Jackson. It had only maimed him. Dr. Hunter McGuire was left no option but to amputate the General's left arm. James did not know McGuire personally, however, he had often seen him at Jackson's side tending various ailments. If Stonewall was to survive the wound, his best chance lay in the skilled hands of his personal physician.

James found some comfort in the fact that men he considered much weaker than Stonewall Jackson, including himself, had survived losing a limb or some other traumatizing wound.

James stayed just a few hundred yards behind the front most of the night, helping the wounded who were able to walk in their journey toward the rear. Around four o'clock in the morning, a surgeon solicited his help and asked him to serve in the capacity of an orderly. At the hospital tent, James witnessed what the Johnsons must have experienced with him. Here the cases were much more severe. He stayed until sun up, in spite of the constant nausea and weariness from his sleepless travel. He saw hundreds of arms and legs amputated and stacked outside the tent to be left for the flies and buzzards.

During those hellish, few hours, the horse Mr. Johnson had

gotten for him, which he simply referred to as Pal, remained safe and calm in a clump of dense woods directly behind the surgeon's tent. At daybreak, James was surprised to find that no one had decided to relieve him of Pal and ride out the fight. More probably, the animal had gone unnoticed.

The next day brought with it more fighting, killing, and maiming. James wished he was at the front so he could escape the explicit view of the carnage. From what he saw there, James knew that death, in all its finality, was a blessing to many. One man he saw had lost both of his legs and was pulling himself along the ground with his arms. James ran for the man as soon as he saw him, but, before he could get there, the man died. James found a very calm expression on that man's grimy face. Under the dirt, he could see, pain had left forever.

Jeb Stuart was put in charge of Jackson's "foot cavalry". Under Stuart's leadership, the troops fought with vengeance. Although Hooker's army survived the fight, only the South's relatively small numbers saved the Yanks from total destruction as a fighting force. Since that time, many have questioned whether the final blow to end the war could have been delivered had Jackson been with his men. It seems doubtful that they could have done much more, given the numerical superiority of the foe, with or without the added presence of the hard driving Stonewall.

James ended the day, as he had begun it, by helping surgeons carve up humanity. The sight of mangled muscle, jaggedly powder fried flesh, and torn bones created a scene which was indelibly etched into the memory of the once confident Confederate.

The last time James saw the tent was shortly after a man had both his legs amputated. The patient had been shot in both limbs simultaneously and vital veins had been destroyed. Without amputation, or proper drugs which were exhausted long before, gangrene would set in, and the man would suffer greatly before inevitably dying. The choice of death or a legless life left little hope. Since there was no chloroform, whisky, or other alternative pain killer available, James usually tried to calm the men with talk before the cutting began. One patient's name was John Jennings. He was from Maury County in Middle Tennessee, which was about twenty miles directly south of Franklin. Ironically, Jennings, who had suffered injuries to his stomach and groin area, was calmer than James. With that ever so slow back-country drawl common to so many of the "regulars," he related his short and extraordinary tale of events leading up to his wounding.

"I joined the Twentieth regiment about four months ago," he began. "Along with about a hundred others from the county. By a couple of days or so ago there were only thirty left, but we still had our flag!"

James was so stunned, he couldn't speak. Jennings was, of course, unaware of any connection between his regiment and this young man helping prepare him for the surgeon's scalpel.

"Right before I was hit, I saw some son of bitch Yank carrying our flag toward the rear, waving it like a damn trophy.

"At that point there was a lull in the fighting, so, the last ten of us set out to get our flag back. I was hit real quick and from where I was laying, I could see all the rest go down. A few minutes after that, Ewell's boys rocked those Yanks hard, right where we went down. If any of the boys are left alive beside me, I hope they got the colors."

He died before James could inform him that James, himself, had once been part of the Twentieth. The surgeons didn't even have to begin cutting before the last painful seconds of life passed for yet another unfortunate victim.

James was unable to speak after that. He was greatly shaken, and mounted Pal and rode, hard. Anywhere. He really didn't care where, just away from the blood. After about a mile, he became nauseated and threw up. The only food he'd eaten in the last three days was parched corn and stale bacon from the hospital tent. That food was his reward for services rendered and a commodity unknown to the soldiers on the front.

In his hurried departure he had not noticed in which direction he had headed. Luckily, it was the right one. As he looked up, all he could see were Yankee prisoners and Confederate wounded. He was headed South.

His indifference toward death and dying had softened. It was different in the rear than at the front, very different. At the front, there wasn't time to deal with anything but the fight. The slightest wandering of the mind or slouching would result in death. It sat squarely in his mind.

He recalled how Harry Larkin had been so relaxed at Shiloh. They probably would have to wait another hour, at least, before they headed for the hornet's nest. Young Harry was stretched out just as comfortable as you please one moment, and the next, he was dead, a hole in the middle of his head. Nobody even heard the shot. James learned the value of being alert at that moment.

It was hard to imagine that the Twentieth had ceased to exist. So many that James had known and grown up with and spent all his life with were gone. They could not be replaced. At that point, James determined to ride for Richmond and make his way home from there.

James arrived in the Confederate capital on May eleven. The city was mysteriously calm and quiet. After a victory such as Chancellorsville, Richmond should have been alive with joy and excitement. Oddly, shades were drawn in almost every house he passed.

He had been through the city only once before, when the Twentieth had been pulled away from Tennessee to reinforce the Army of Northern Virginia in August of 1862. Unbeknownst to anyone, the Twentieth would never return to Tennessee. The first time through the capital, there had been pretty gals and booze everywhere. The streets were overflowing, all just out of the reach of the men. Their view was from a train window, moving much too fast to get even as much as a touch or sip. James had been looking forward to a reproduction of that first visit, but at a slower speed. What he found was in stark contrast to his anticipations.

Then it struck him. Perhaps Jackson had died. All the reports James had heard from the battlefield had been positive about the condition of the man they called "The Stone Wall." James stopped the first person he saw, and found that pneumonia had been the killer. The body would be in town the next day, on its way to lay in state at Virginia Military Institute. No military victory was worth the loss of Stonewall Jackson. He worried that the South would not recover from a blow of such magnitude. The cause could more afford to lose 50,000 fighting men. The Twentieth had fought many times right next to the "foot cavalry" and they were undoubtedly the most agile and powerful unit on either side. Hopefully, these men would rebound.

Not knowing anywhere else to go, James headed for the war department. As he neared the seat of Southern military control, activity in the streets picked up dramatically. People moved about very quickly. The slightly wounded and permanently maimed were most visible. The building next to the war department building had been turned into a hospital, and brought a familiar, yet terrible stench to the whole area.

Inside the war department, James could find no one who would assume responsibility for someone who was thought to be dead. He found, however, that they had already written his father. The copy of the telegram read:

"James Wilson, Jr. died bravely for the South in the Maryland campaign."

James' only hope was that the bad state of affairs which existed in the administration in general affected the postal/telegraph system specifically. If so, that would allow him time to get home before the letter or telegram would be received. There was so much confusion at the war department that the letter had only been sent a week earlier, which meant it probably had not left the building. He had to hurry on. If the mails/telegraph ran at all, his demise would be announced. He hoped there would be survivors who would care.

As he left, James looked back and wondered how this government ever accomplished anything. The government's seat was a city of high prices and profiteering in every conceivable market from horse flesh to human flesh. Since the beginning of the war, Richmond's population had swelled fourfold to 40,000 inhabitants including a large percentage of prostitutes and hangers-on of every variety. Even though exorbitant prices were charged for the daily necessities, the people continued to pay. When it came to food, the choice was simple, pay the price or don't eat.

At the train depot, the crowd was gigantic. Wounded were arriving by rail every half hour. James found that for $400 Confederate or written orders from that same confused war department, he could take an arduously long journey through the deep South and arrive in middle Tennessee in four or five days. He would travel through Virginia, North Carolina, Georgia, and Alabama, finally ending his journey in Tullahoma, Tennessee, about forty miles southeast of Franklin. James didn't have $400 and nobody was writing orders for a dead man. He didn't own anything to sell with the exception of his horse and saddle, which wouldn't bring $50.00, and in fact weren't really his.

He had to move on. He couldn't sit there and wait even though it would give him the chance to see Stonewall's remains and a little Richmond gaiety. He headed straight for the southwestern outskirts of the city in order to start the long ride home. He picked up some supplies going through town from a populace who seemed ambivalent to the prices being paid. The selection was enormous, however at exorbitant prices. A lady gave him two cooked chickens and two loaves of bread. An elderly man gave him a bottle of brandy and a covered jar of jam while the man at the livery shod Pal for free and gave James two saddlebags full of oats. It made James want to stay but he knew these people were in for a fall, and he didn't want to be there when it finally came.

James figured he could make the trip in about one week if he and Pal could stand the pace. The shortest route was directly southwest through East Tennessee. Unfortunately, that section was Yankee held and Yankee loved. That course was therefore out of the question. The other alternative was to head due south through North Carolina, then turn west toward North Georgia, then northwest to Middle Tennessee, and finally home. This trip would mirror the Confederate rail trip, but on an inside course. At best, on horseback, it would be a ten-day journey.

As James left the outskirts of Richmond, the realities of war struck at him like a snake that had been lying in wait in the back of his mind waiting for the right opportunity to rear its ugly head. The railroad system was in shambles. All ordinance areas of the war were deficient, from shoes to cannon. Yet, the people remained as generous as ever. Prices were high and rising. Manufacturing capacity was declining as destroyed mills could not be replaced yet the people continued to give.

Conditions in North Carolina were horrible, and even worse in North Georgia. Neither could compare to the devastation in Southeastern Tennessee which had been picked over for three years alternately by Northern and Southern troops as the tides of war ebbed and flowed. Even though Chattanooga was still held by the South, its hold was slipping every day as invading armies inched closer and closer.

Following seven days and six nights of almost constant travel, James stopped and looked down upon Chattanooga from Lookout Mountain, across the Tennessee River from the growing little town. He rested for half of a day, traded Pal for an animal which looked and acted more like a mule than anything else, and set out for Tullahoma, the northernmost Confederate stronghold in Middle Tennessee.

From Chattanooga, he found conditions to be much worse than he had expected. Food of any description was extremely scarce. War conditions, the absence of most of the men for planting and harvesting crops, and constant raids from Yankee cavalry left the people living on very little indeed.

East of Tullahoma, James stopped at a small log farm house to water and rest himself and his mount. The farm was owned by a family named Quinn. Only two small boys and their mother, Rebecca, remained there. The mother offered James a place to sleep in addition to all the water he could pull out of the well. Embarrassingly, all she could offer in the way of food were greens and yams. As sparse as her supply was, she gave freely.

Finding that he had come from Richmond, Rebecca questioned James about her husband Martin, of the Seventh Virginia Cavalry. She had not heard from him since he joined up almost two years earlier.

"Martin is smart," she said, "he bought this farm about five years ago, when we lived in Alexandria. He had been an architect in Washington.

"He knew trouble was coming, but, he thought we could come out here and get away from it. He never realized how big the fight would be.

"When it came, I knew he'd have to go. After he left we came on West ourselves, me and the boys."

When James told her that he knew nothing of her husband, she couldn't hide her disappointment.

"We'll just wait and get by somehow until we win the war and Martin comes home," she vowed.

Rebecca Quinn made James more determined than ever before. If she could go on hoping against hope for two years and more, surely nothing was lost. As James was leaving, he thanked Mrs. Quinn.

"I can't predict the future, but I promise this thing is far from over. I hope God blesses you with the safe return of your husband," he prayed. As he mounted and left, the impression of that woman and her sons, standing resolutely in front of their cabin, was stamped into his mind, never to be forgotten.

From Tullahoma on, everything got real tight. James saw very few people. Those he did see were mostly shadows, like himself, not inclined to stop or slow down enough to see who might be passing. Others were too scared to show themselves. He was lucky, insofar as he saw no Yankee patrols until he got to Spring Hill on the morning of the seventeenth.

There were plenty of Yanks in that area which meant Franklin, just ten miles farther north, was also alive with the boys in blue. The Federals in the Spring Hill area were on the move southward and were most probably the beginning of a new offensive. There were too many for James to leave his hiding place in the woods until nightfall. He sat, waited, and watched. Being so close to home, just ten miles up the Franklin Pike, made the day pass slowly. Impatiently, James waited for darkness, knowing that with the cover of nightfall, he could ride the short distance blindfolded, for no one knew the area better than he. While he sat, he counted twelve full regiments of Northern arms of all types, almost 10,000 men, headed south. There sure as hell was something going on.

After nightfall, he began his ride. Around nine o'clock that night, James knew that he was approaching his own property. He had made good time and, finally reached home. Still he was in the woods and the moon was full, so, he decided to wait again until after midnight.

James was sitting on top of Winstead Hill. The hill, which rose about two hundred feet, was about a mile directly south of his house. From where he was, James could see and hear any activity that might materialize on the road below him. At three o'clock a.m. he started north, to the left of the road about 100 yards or so along a curving line of evergreens.

James knew where he was for he had ridden that same path thousands of times in his youth. In his fatigued condition, his mind tricked him into thinking he saw the ruins of his home. He realized, quickly, that his house was not visible from his vantage point, be it day or night due to the fact that there was a rise in the ground which would hide his house from view. The panic and accompanying anxiety overpowered the journeyman.

About a hundred yards out, he saw a light and the silhouette of a house. Still there was no movement from anywhere, without or within. That made sense for that time of the morning. He was amazed to find fresh whitewash on the two fence rows that came together at the edge of the yard fifty feet from the house. He didn't expect to find them standing, especially in such condition. Something had to be wrong. He leaned back against the familiar south wall to check his Colt. He asked himself how things could be in such good shape at his home while gross inadequacies dominated the rest of the South. James began to expect real trouble as he crept toward the long side porch facing west from the house.

Chapter 4
Reunion/Yankees

As he ran hunched over from the hip, James saw a movement in the third window of the long veranda which stopped him dead in his tracks. He saw two people talking, one was white, the other black. James was very quiet as he got right up under the window sill where he identified the black man as his life long friend, Jacob. The white man wore Confederate grey, which might explain why he was there so late at night. James had never seen the officer before.

In his mind he questioned the whereabouts of his father and why Jacob was in the house while his father was not. As far as James knew, no one, white or black, had ever been in the Wilson home alone, except Jesse Mai, who was Jacob's mother and James' nanny. There was only one way to answer all the questions running through James' mind. He pulled his Colt and knife, ran the length of the porch, and broke in through the side door.

The moment Jacob saw his long lost friend, he dropped a silver tray filled with bread and a pitcher of milk. An aura of peace overtook James as the familiar surroundings welcomed him. He felt as if he was dreaming. He swore he even smelled real coffee. Things inside were even better than they had looked from the outside. That was perplexing insomuch as here in Yankee held territory, his people wanted for nothing. James continued to point his gun at the officer, unsure of who or what or even how many he was confronting, assuming that Jacob might have changed his allegiance to that of the Union Flag.

After a few moments, which seemed like hours, Jacob began to spout forth disbelief and blessings at the same time. As he rushed to James, he almost tripped on the fallen tray, but regained his balance to hug James. James then knew that he was safe.

Jacob identified the Confederate officer as W.L. Duckworth of the Seventh Tennessee cavalry commanded by Nathan Forrest. Duckworth had just arrived with the news of James' demise. Since James' dad was not home, no one else knew of the erroneous report of the soldier's death. James sank down in one of the newly upholstered dining room chairs to find some air and gather himself.

"Where is my father? Why is everything in such good shape? And fresh milk? People in this country would kill for that and there it sits on the floor of my homes' immaculately furnished dining room. How? There are Yankees all over the damn place," he rambled.

Colonel Duckworth started to respond, but was cut off by Jacob.

"Yo daddy gots im a real deal wid dem Yankees. He lets em hole a lot a hosses an cows yere wid all kines of uddah stuff d' army's need."

James was filled with disbelief and knew it showed.

"In retuhn, in de front, d' Yanks makes sho 'at nuttin happens yere and keeps us full supplied," the slave continued. "Sho beats me how stupid doze yanks kin be. A good paht uf all dat comes yere goes on souf ta d' Ginral. An yea knows Missa James hous I feel 'bout ole Forrest. Him n' yo daddy saved me an my famly from bein' split up. Anyhows, yo daddy aint yere cause he lef on de las trip souf t' take stock an such ta de Ginral. He be gitten home anyday, an will he be sho glad t' see yea."

Such a fantastic story was hard for James to swallow. Having known Jacob all his life, he knew it must be true. Jacob, like James, had always been straight forward and honest. He had to believe his black friend. He turned to Duckworth who began before James could speak.

"Your father really has the Yanks so lost that they don't know that they are being taken advantage of. He decided that the only way to secure his property and family, other than you, was to sympathize, or, at least appear to sympathize with the Feds. He took it one step further to help the Confederacy as well. It's really a great ploy.

"Your father went to Gordon Granger, the ranking Union officer in this area, stated his allegiance and demanded protection. All this, of course, was known by General Forrest.

"He succeeded much better than he ever thought he would. He and Granger even appear to be close. Granger himself proposed that the Feds keep their inventory at your place, as it was best suited for animals and storage. That was just what your father wanted to happen. He even arranged for all the bookkeeping to be done by him and his work is never checked or questioned."

James could barely speak from the shock.

"I can't believe what I'm hearing. Could this be some sort of dream?"

"It's no dream, son" Duckworth replied, "Your father has sacrificed a great deal. Most of your neighbors don't know the true situation either, and therefore, feel that your father is a traitor. He's lost almost no personal property. Right before the Feds took control of this area, your father had everything of value, except the beefstock at Forrest's request, converted to cash.

"The people on the farm were all given hard cash for all they were due, farm necessities were deducted, and the balance, around $20,000, was invested in England through some Californians your father had helped with horseflesh before the war. Then, he went to see Granger. The rest is past. Everybody's happy. The Yanks have a well run ordinance system. We get ample supplies, regularly. And your father's property is protected. Which brings us back to you. I was sent here to report the bad news of your death. How did that happen?"

"I was wounded, shot up real bad at Antietam," James began,

"and left for dead. I was found by a man and his daughter from Frederick, Maryland. They, the Johnsons, nursed me back to health.

"The most ironic and unbelievable part of my past half-year existence is that that family, the Johnsons, lost a son right across from where they found me. I might even have been the one who killed him before I went down myself. The daughter, is a young girl named Camille. I'm going to go back for her...someday."

"In love with a Yankee. Wait till your father hears about that," Duckworth laughed uproariously.

"On my way here, I went through Chancellorsville the night of the first day," James continued. "It was horrible and I couldn't fight, so I helped with the wounded. I will never be in the rear during a battle again. My stomach just can't take it. It was a sad day.

"In Richmond, the people were either jubilant or totally defeated. From there I headed south through Danville and North Carolina, west into North Georgia and Chattanooga, and from there northwest to Tullahoma and here. I didn't find much 'give up' in the people I ran into along the way.

"Hell, one woman I met has two little boys and hasn't heard from her husband in over two years. She has no money and no prospects, but refuses to quit. And I feel the same way, dammit . I can't march or fight on foot, but I can ride and my leg's getting better everyday. Somehow, I'm getting back into it."

The whole time James was talking, Jacob was grinning and laughing while cleaning up the mess from the fallen tray and pitcher. As he finished gathering all of the debris he smiled at James.

"Dem Yanks tried t' git everbody t' run awf. Not a singul one is gawn t'day," he said. "Deys all know days beddah awf right yere wid yo daddy. Eben if dey twerent no wah, we couldn't do no beddah dan we is. We alls knows we's free wid d' papers fuh proof. Don yaw wuhri nun 'bout any d' people yere. Wew all t'gethah. All de stock, hawsses, pigs, cows, and de like is hid in d' valley 'bout three miles over at Cahtahs Creek. Dem dumb Yanks aint foun it, dey aint eben looked its so close to em."

Duckworth added, "The Yanks aren't very particular about their possessions. One fourth of everything that passes through here, heads straight south to General Forrest."

By then, James was also grinning and laughing. His family had the best that could ever be possible, right in the middle of a situation that could not possibly be worse. His house still stood, in Yankee held territory, the farm still worked and even made a few bucks, in Yankee held territory; all the Wilson people were alive, well, and together, in Yankee held territory; and the cause of the Confederacy was being well served, in Yankee held territory.

"Well, Colonel, how really does this not become obvious to the Feds?"

"First of all, you must understand that no one in Franklin or anywhere else knows of this arrangement. Most people here see your father as a traitor, and you must do nothing to dispel their illusion. If anyone other than us finds out, it will be impossible to keep the word from spreading," said Duckworth very emphatically. "Secondly, to answer how this all really works, I defer to your friend Jacob."

"Y' knows, James, dat de bes man wid a haws in dis necka d' woods is me. Well, dem damn yanks fo some reason make mount schanges at night. Yo daddys pinted me as dwone t' handle de schange. I jes grab up a bunch of d' used ones and keep on headin souf t' hook up wid de Kuhnul yere n' his min," Jacob jawed.

"The farm is so efficient, it actually saves the Yanks money. The Wilson plantation is the best known ordinance center in the state. It's only a matter of time before Jacob here or some others are caught headed south with livestock branded U.S. So, we have to be very careful," Duckworth added.

James was wonderstruck. He could not fathom what he'd heard. In spite of all the good news, he was very concerned about the whereabouts and well being of his father. Duckworth was very convincing about Mr. Wilson's safety and his story was in keeping with the others of which James had just learned.

"Whenever your dad and the General finish their business,

whether it be yesterday, today, or tomorrow, your father will be accompanied as far as Tullahoma by Forrest and his escort company.

"From Tullahoma to Columbia or maybe Spring Hill your father will travel alone for about thirty five miles. From there he will allow himself to be picked up by Federal cavalry who will bring him right to the doorstep." Duckworth, who could hardly contain himself, continued.

"Those Yanks will ride almost onto the porch to deliver their valuable associate safely. It's just a damn amazing situation. As a result, your father is solely responsible for one and one-half years of helping feed and mount thousands of men that our government, otherwise, could not provide for."

"I have one final question. Then I'll try to catch up on some sleep. What happens when the Yanks catch on here?" he asked. "It has to happen one day."

"Real straight shooter, ain't ya boy?" Duckworth grimaced.

"One, don't call me boy. And two, your damn right its gonna be straight," James shot back, as anger swelled up in his neck and his frame straightened upright.

As close as he had come to death on the front, in addition to the contributions his family had made away from the front, he knew he would never reach for compromise with any man, ever again. Duckworth was no fool. He was a colonel under Forrest, which commanded James' respect. If Duckworth was capable enough for Forrest to trust him with command of a full regiment, including the General's personal escort, James would allow him the appropriate respect.

"Unless captured immediately, your father should easily get out with whatever he can take with him. Since the Federals have no knowledge of the existence of the hidden stock, the hands can leave gradually and quietly probably taking a good bit with them. So, except for this house, which really isn't worth much in this situation, what have we got to lose?"

"And if my father is captured?"

"He will be hanged. Be assured."

Duckworth knew how those words stung the young Wilson. But, it was straight talk, and that was what was called for.

At that, James rose, headed for the door, turned and asked where he should stay. It was a strange feeling for him to have to ask as to where he should stay in his own home. Jacob led James straight away up the steps above the kitchen to a hidden room in the attic. There had been many times in earlier years when James had hidden out up there to avoid an annoying chore. Therefore, he knew it well.

It wasn't really much of a room. More of a cubby hole really, maybe eight feet by fifteen feet. Actually it was more comfortable now thanks to a down mattress and plenty of fresh air from a hole Jim Wilson had cut into the side of the house in anticipation of his son's homecoming.

"I'm sure glad to be home," James sighed as he slipped onto the mattress.

"And we damn glad yo hea," replied his friend. "G'nite Missa James."

James turned quickly to grab Jacob's arm before he left the room, and said "From here on, no more mister, unless, of course, you want me mistering you. You're a free man. You're my own age. And you're my friend, and we don't mister anymore, ok?"

Jacob, somewhat amazed at a side of his friend he had never seen, nodded his agreement and turned to leave.

"G'nite James," he suggested.

The words fell upon slumbering ears as James was already fast asleep, overcome by physical exertion and mental fatigue.

As usual, morning came early for James. Sleep had been elusive, even with the comforts of home and a fatigue that penetrated the soul. The insomnia was caused by a damn large measure of anxiety. Shortly before sunup, he had risen and left the house. He wanted to thoroughly inspect the place and take care of his hybrid mount which he had left standing and saddled the night before. He looked for his mule which was nowhere to be found, then headed straight to the barn.

As the sun began to rise over the river toward Murfreesboro, there was much more to be seen than the night before. The barn and all the other outbuildings, including the worker's quarters still stood strong and straight. They had been very well maintained. In the barn, six of the fourteen stalls were occupied. The animals seemed strong and healthy. Nothing like the livestock to which he had recently become accustomed. The horses in the Confederate army were mere skeletons compared to what he found in his family's stables. They were all branded "U.S."

James found his mule, safe and sound, tethered up to the back of the barn. He climbed to the top rail of the fencing that formed a corral in back of the building to look the place over. There, James' heart pounded furiously as he thought about the days that were forever gone and hoped for his father's safe return. His throat began to close as his mind moved on to Maryland.

He had survived and was better off than he should be considering what he'd been through. He thought of Camille and Poppy. It wasn't like before the war when he would have been able to write back and forth forming a courtship of sorts. He feared he might never see her again. Her potential absence from his life depressed him so badly that he decided to try to erase the memory of the time in Frederick from his confused mind.

Old Mai had begun stirring up some breakfast around sun up, so he put his mule out of sight and headed back toward the house. He could surprise her if word of his arrival had not found a resting place in her ear during the night. As he approached the house he realized his attempts to shake his thoughts of Camille had proven unsuccessful. This lack of success was reassuring as it reinforced his love for her.

Before he was halfway there, James was surrounded by the people he had grown up with and had missed for so long. None were white. Smiles and hugs and kisses came from every direction and every gender. They didn't care and neither did he. Since he was a little boy, he and his father had always had touching, physical relationships with their people. Jacob's kin folks, which included all the blacks on the farm, knew the kind of touching the Wilsons did meant love. There was never physical punishment or any attempt to break their spirit.

Everyone was at breakfast, including Mai's brother Jim, who was unable to move too well mainly because of his rheumatism and partly due to just plain old age. James figured Uncle Jim had to be in his mid-eighties by that Summer of 1863.

James found Mai way past the getting ready stage for breakfast. Quarter-inch-thick slabs of ham were frying, biscuits and cakes were stacked high on the big mahogany topped kitchen table, and a platter of scrambled eggs was resting on a new warming device right beside the stove, absorbing its excess heat. The table which was imported from California when James was around ten years old was a full fifteen yards long and two across, accommodating everyone on the farm at once on rare occasions like Christmas. Mai had her daughters, Suzy and Bee, helping about the kitchen. The minute her eyes saw her baby approach the door, she handed her spatula to Bee and headed for some smothering.

And smother she did! Her weight doubled that of James and he never stood a chance. She raised him right off of the floor. In addition to the smell of food, he smelled "real" coffee, an aroma James had not sensed in the two years while in the army was once again brewing. In the army, the only coffee served was made from ground hickory nuts or walnuts. The concoction was served warm which was its only semblance to real coffee.

Mai sat James down on the table, poured him a cup of the nectar, and, stood back in order to admire him.

"Laud, boy, we's bin missin ya." Mai was grinning from ear to ear as were Suzy and Bee who both had to get in their own hugs. They were about the same age as James' mother would have been had she been alive. Mai just kept right on during all the commotion.

"Whhah y' bin and why so long? An yo so small an gimpy," she noted. "Is dat permanut? Lawd, chile, it don't mattah nun. Ya home an safe an I don't knows how y' pappy do it but somehow he got dem Yankees tricked an we's beddah awf dan eber. Y' should hab been widdus de whole time. Well, can't y' eben talk or did dey shoot ya in dmouf er sumpun?"

James' eyes were wet when he said, "I just can't believe what I've found here, Mai. Particularly compared to what I've seen in the other places I've been," he whispered behind his tears, "including the Army."

"As I sade, I doan rilly unnerstan how y' fadda dun wut he dun, but I does know dat moze de neighbahs, 'specially dose who laws boys so fah, ain't reall neighbahs no mo, if y' knows wuts I mean," Mai interjected. "De don't come callin no mo, liken de used ta. An now, we kin hep em."

"Someday, Mai," James continued, "We'll explain all of what's happening here to everyone. In the meantime, keep doing what you are and let me tell you where I've been and what I've seen.

"I couldn't come home at first because of army rules. Then I got shot up pretty bad way up north of here in Maryland. But, a wonderful man and his daughter took me in, kept me from being captured and thrown in prison, and nursed me back to health. And I, uh, I think I fell in love with a Yankee girl."

As James tried to wrap his little arms around Mai again, he realized that she was the closest thing to a real mother he had ever had.

"I sure have missed you Aunt Mai."

"An me too chile."

Jacob had come in in the middle of James' and Mai's talk and was sitting drinking coffee with real cream and sugar, just listening and grinning.

"None uzun really unnerstan dis deal yo daddy got but we knows it makes him look bad ta de neighahs, so tween dem an de Yanks y' got to stay low long as y' heah. But, we's all glad y' home an we'll take care of ya, limp and all.

"By de way, some months back a Yank Capain come by an he say dat dere President Linkum dun freed all black fokes in d' whole Souf. We didn't pay him much mine seein we already free an makin money, but what did it mean?"

James thought for a few moments and then tried to explain. Beside Jacob, his brothers Willie and young Jim, several others were hanging in the door and on the table just to get a look at James and maybe a chance to talk with him and offer welcomes. They all listened intently to James' answer.

"Basically, President Lincoln has stated that after January 1, of this year, which was of course, several months back, he considers any and all slaves, most of the blacks in the South, and especially those in states at war with his government to be free. And when his armies enter the South like they are here, he hopes those slaves will leave their masters and homes thereby crippling the output of the big farms that have managed to remain in existence here."

"But what he gonna do wid dem peoples?" Jacob asked with a real puzzling look on his face. "See, some has run off from roun heah. An ebry now an den win we goes ta Nashville to hep transpote Yankee supplies to heah, I sees a few of dem. An dey an't got nuttin ta do an jes wander aroun. An wid nuttin to do y' knows de aint got no money."

"Jacob, that part I don't rightly know how to answer, but I do know that it will hurt the South."

"I giss," Jacob continued, "dat mos people haint neah as smaht as y' fadda in makin us all free an makin money sometime ago. Til yo daddy gets hisself caught doin what he's doin, we'll be right heah wid him. An win he got to go we be right dare wid him too."

Everyone in the room nodded their agreement to Jacob's words. Then Mai took over, just like she always had.

"Now all ya'll get gone on to wuk. James eat some of dis good food fo it goes bad and hurry up to meet da Kuhnel. He needs ta tell y' bout de place. But, fo y' go tell me bout huh, de girl up Nawf. Is she pretty as Franklin gals?" Mai inquired.

"Who?," James stammered, turning as red as blood.

"Y' knows who," Mai grinned.

"I reckon this war has taught me a lot, Mai. Not anything like I learned from you and Pa, but something a might different.

"White or black, North or South, we shouldn't be killing each other," he continued. "The South, our homes and everything in this society is crumbling right before our eyes. Nobody else in the South still lives the way it is here. Cities are being looted and burned and all the young boys like me are being killed or crippled like I have been.

"In reality, we haven't got a chance. The North has more people and more supplies. Hell, they've got just more of everything. One of these days we will be one country again, I hope.

"Since we don't have a chance of winning the fight, it seems silly to be killing off all the good from both sides. I know it, and you can be sure there are others who know it both here and there. Like the Johnson family, for example, and Camille, that's her name, the girl who nursed me back to health after Sharpsburg.

"Anyway, these Yankee folks saved my life after our army had left me for dead. All in spite of finding a son and brother dead right across the trench from where they found me. In my heart I know I didn't kill him. Probably his own army's artillery fire killed him while crippling me.

"My feelings about this whole thing have changed a lot, cause on top of everything else, I guess I, ah, fell in love with the Johnsons and especially Camille. She's more beautiful than anybody in the world, 'cept maybe you."

James could tell he was really making an impression. He went on, "She's blond, just natural as can be with wide blue eyes and skin so soft. She's not a big gal but she spends a lot of time in her daddy's fields and can ride as good as Jacob. Her complexion is very light somehow," he described. "She's tender yet also strong and firm. I knew I was gonna live the first time I heard her voice and opened my eyes and saw that smile. Words can't do her justice. You'll just have to wait till you see her."

"Well, den, win will 'at be?" asked Mai.

"Probably awhile from now," James answered. "Not till the

fighting ends. I sure hope it's soon, but even so, I've got to go back to it. I can't sit here and wait it out, not with the Yankees taking over our way of life. I have to get back to the fight. By some miracle maybe me and others like me might make a difference."

"Well boy," she said, "Don't y' worry nun bout inny uv us. Includin' yo daddy. He's so much smahter dan everbody else round hea and does moe to boot. Wherever and winever he has ta leave dis place, he'll have plinny o' cumpny. An we jes boun ta go innyweah."

"But Mai, you just don't understand," James pleaded, "Ya'll can't not count on him forever. My father could be captured or even killed for what's he's doing. And where would that leave you?"

"Not much wuhse awf 'n you. I seen y' limpin up heah frum de bahn. How you spect ta git roun er fight like dat?"

"On a horse, that's how," James responded quickly.

"But, win y' daddy do see ya, he woan let y' go back," she prophesied.

"He'll understand and he'll let me go," James whispered as he pulled her massive body down on the bench next to him.

"Well, mebbie I wont," she replied.

James ate quickly and left to find Colonel Duckworth. He found him in the dining room seated directly across the table from his friend, Jacob. What a strange sight James witnessed. There were scores of men in the Confederate army fighting just to keep such a scene from ever taking place anywhere in the South. It resembled some high level war conference between a white and a black against other whites. Although the conversation was not about war, James figured that integration was the shape of things to come. Neither Duckworth or Jacob knew that they were helping to bring that day closer as they fought to preserve something that they both knew, but would not admit, was dying.

"When will my father be here?" James asked.

"Tonight or tomorrow night," Duckworth responded. "He's at least as smart as you, and I didn't meet you, James my boy, in the light of day. Your father, also, knows just about all the Federals stationed permanently in this area. There are also a lot of Yankee units passing through headed south to southeast probably with some trigger happy young fool just eager enough to pick up someone like your dad as a spy or such. Particularly, south of Spring Hill. Even your dad isn't safe from the Feds in that area. Still, I've got a worthless Confederate dollar that says we see him tonight."

The Colonel's words put James' mind to rest somewhat, so he changed the subject.

"What do I need to know about the place? I don't know how long I'll be here, but, as long as I am, I need to know what's what," he demanded.

"Probly, de bes ting fo y' ta do," replied Jacob, "is jes stay inside and away from dat windah y' lookin out uv now."

James jumped back as if bitten by a snake, a move which caused his two companions to belly laugh right out loud. They knew that Jim Wilson somehow had the Yanks totally intimidated about coming on the property unannounced. After more laughter at the expense of the newcomer, Jacob continued.

"I'se take cah of dat hoss uv yose er wutebba it is. Looks mo like mule ta me. An jus keep on runnin de place jes de same. De Kuhnal hea aint leavin till yo daddy gits back nohow. So, you kin stay hid tagethah. He know wat ta do an' wheah ta go iffen inny Yanks do pull in. Now, I gotta get ta it. It'll be a real cho gittin dat ride of yoin out ta pasture widout any trouble."

"But he rides real smooth," James laughed as Jacob left the room.

After Jacob had left, James and Duckworth began talking about the war. James related all the deprivations he had seen coming from Richmond. Duckworth had seen and experienced, except for personal crippling, about the same. He was impressed with the young Wilson's fortitude. He was so impressed that he suggested that General Forrest would be well served by James' intelligence and clear determination. James, too, was awed at the prospect of riding with the likes of his old acquaintance, Bedford Forrest.

His memory took him back several years to a time when N.B. Forrest had been such a help to his father. The man was probably as close to educationally illiterate as possible. It proved to be no hindrance. He ran his whole life on instinct and plain common sense, which wasn't quite so common in the Confederate hierarchy.

"We operate an awful lot in this area on raids and such. So, if you can really ride well enough to keep up and, most importantly, keep on living, you'll always be just an order away from home," Duckworth Colonelled, which added more appeal to the opportunity.

The two talked for the rest of the morning and most of the afternoon. By three or four o'clock, the anxiety of awaiting his father's return sent James once again to the down mattress in the hidden cubicle. Exhausted, he lay down feeling as safe and protected as if it were fifteen years before. He was asleep in a matter of minutes and did not awaken until the sun had been up for a couple of hours the next day. It was the first peaceful rest he had experienced in at least two years.

Climbing out of bed, he heard activity below. Realizing that it was early morning, James knew that what he heard was not his father's arrival. He would have already been awakened for that event. Once again, he found the source of the noise to be Jacob and Duckworth, which meant that the day would be spent like the last, cooped up with impatience and restlessness, thinking and wondering what would it be like to take part in active operations with Forrest in the Middle Tennessee area so close to home. It just didn't make sense. If James knew the score, surely a man like General Forrest also understood that the South was not winning. Was he right to risk his life a second and, maybe final time for a cause that, he reasoned, must have been long lost even before then. He was damn lucky to be alive in the first place. He wondered if he should tempt fate.

The odds were very long and stacked against him. Being part of Forrest's command would subject him to life threatening situations on a constant basis. James had heard and read that some of the General's men, who had been captured, were hanged as spies by order of the Yankee General, Sherman, who was greatly disturbed by the successes achieved by Forrest and his command behind Federal lines.

If Forrest wasn't quitting, maybe there was something that James was missing or just didn't understand. He knew that the Confederate armies were virtually reduced to rags. Southern civilians were generally destitute with little, if any, real money, and the Yanks were inching farther and farther south, capturing more and more territory all the time.

"Dammit, why don't those sons-of-bitches just go away and leave us alone?" James didn't even realize that he had yelled.

Duckworth, creeping up the stairs to be sure that he was awake was answering all the same.

"They can't do that anymore than we can just roll over and play dead for them. A lot is at stake for them too. After all, we fired the first shot, like a bunch of hotheads, otherwise, they might have let us go in peace," he explained. "Besides that, as you know, they've got everything on their side - men, machinery of war, provisions, and all the other materials needed to wage a successful war effort.

"All that we have going for us is that our backs are against the wall, and we're fighting for our homes and family's safety. And, dammit, James, you must know that when a man's fighting for his home and family, he's rattlesnake mean. Mean enough to not give up no matter what the odds. However, I've been spared wounds such as yours. I doubt very seriously that I have been through as much living hell as you and your father and persisted.

"Especially the mental abuse your father has taken becuase of the way Granger and the rest think he is a Unionist alone in a sea of secessionists. He's been able to perpetrate this whole scheme, allowing himself to be hated as a traitor while serving his beloved Confederacy. I don't believe that Nathan Bedford Forrest respects any man as much as he does your father.

"All these people here know what a successful Confederate

war effort would mean to their race. With few exceptions, slavery would continue even though Jacob, Mai, Uncle James and all the rest are free anyway.

"They know what has been done for them and if the South could win this war, men such as your father would continue fighting to make all men free. You my friend, just have to make up your own mind and learn to live with your decision. I know how your father feels. Short of giving up his life, the sacrifice of his good name is the greatest gift he could give. We all know that this hoodwink can't last forever. Sooner or later, the Yanks are bound to get wise to what's happening here. We are prepared to get out when the time comes."

James wiped his hands across his face as if he could rub away this awful situation as he would a headache.

"This place here, right here, it's my home," he declared.

"All the Duckworths are up around Lexington, Kentucky," the Colonel lamented. "I have no idea how my wife is at home, or my two sons who were last seen riding with Fitz Lee somewhere in Virginia.

"I was really hoping the other day when we met that you might somehow have known John and Campbell, my boys. I suppose you would have told me if you had any information. Its been since the start of the war that I received any news from them. Miracles or something real close have been known to happen. Being around the good General, really makes me believe. I've seen him do some damn miraculous things with the limited resources which he has available to him, even with your father's help."

Early in the afternoon, Mai brought them lunch which was provided entirely at Yankee expense. Once again, James could not believe his eyes. The meal consisted of bread, ham, real butter, smoked oyster, pickles, real coffee, and sugar. The bloated men topped off the meal with genuine Cuban cigars. One bad habit that James had not picked up during his army life was smoking. After this cigar experience, he doubted that he would acquire the vice.

At the height of James' coughing spell, Duckworth spotted

a Yankee patrol headed south on Columbia Pike. Then he and James prepared to leave the front of the house for more clandestine accommodations.

"Dey has kep on goin. Don't ya'll worry none. Missa Wilson's got em ta scared to jes drop in, uninvited," Mai reported.

At that, they all laughed and sat down to relax and plan events to come. With Federal patrols combing the area, the Colonel thought they should still get away from the front of the house. They followed Mai to the kitchen, knowing that Jacob would take care of anything in blue that came up the long drive from Columbia Pike.

When they got to the kitchen, Duckworth pulled out a map of Middle Tennessee, North Alabama, and North Georgia to brief James on the movements of the troops and to show him where his father and Forrest's command was most likely to be operating.

Before they could focus on the map, the Colonel extended his hand to James enclosing a crumpled Confederate $10 bill.

"I don't believe I've paid off yet," he confessed.

"The wager was only a dollar and I guess you know that I don't have change," James retorted.

"Yes, yes," the Colonel admitted, "but this includes interest from this morning plus inflation which has probably taken more than I've accounted for. I really thought we'd see your father last night. Not that I'm worried about him or anything. Something urgent must have come up with General Forrest to cause the delay.

"I've stated time and time again, your father knows better than anyone how to take care of himself. Don't you worry about him. He'll be here when he can. Now take this worthless money and let me show you some things on this map."

He drew a circle around the Tuscumbia, Alabama, region, just southeast of the Tennessee River.

"This is where your father and the General usually meet to transfer stock and provisions. Probably all the resources that your father took south on this trip have been put to good use against the Yanks in one way or another. I don't know what other business could be causing the prolonged stay. I suspect, however, that they decided to wait before returning because of the Federal build up you saw on your way home."

Then he drew a straight line from Tuscumbia to Tullahoma, Tennessee, where Bragg's main Confederate force was concentrated.

"The two bodies of troops at the ends of this line, Forrest and Bragg, respectively, are the only organized troops of any size in the entire area available to slow any advance that might be coming.

"As the last major city in the state in our hands, Chattanooga is most vital to our cause. You can damn well believe that the Yanks want to take it as badly as we want to keep it. They need it as a base of supply for any thrust into Georgia. To compound our problem, we cannot concentrate all of our forces in the Lookout Mountain area without sacrificing Alabama and all its valuable resources and manufacturing capacity.

"Right now there is a line about eighty to a hundred miles long, connecting North Alabama with Middle Tennessee, covering Chattanooga as well.

"The problem is that Forrest is a fighter and Bragg, well, Bragg may not possess the killer instinct. The impression that I have from Forrest is that the line of resistance is already too thin and is growing more so every day. The reason, according to the General, is timidness. General Forrest does not hold much faith in Bragg's abilities and has said as much, even to Bragg himself.

"The war department and the President support Bragg as the departmental commander and blindly trust his detached judgement.

"As for me, I have more faith in Nathan Forrest than any man in the entire Confederate Army. I surely wish that he was in command. If he was, I can't help but think that the Federals would have been viciously attacked on all fronts and Tennessee would still be in our hands."

"Even taking into account the weight of numbers in favor of the North?" James inquired.

Duckworth had a wiry kind of smile that drooped at the corners of his mouth and joined his mustache giving him the appearance of a walrus. He was smiling just that way, sort of underneath looking, when he answered.

"I guess you know that the General doesn't know too damn much about numbers. Even if he did, I doubt very seriously that his nature would let him call it quits."

He also had in his possession at the time a copy of the most recent edition of the Franklin weekly newspaper and two other dailies from Nashville. As expected, with Union occupation, all were biased with Union views of the war. A great deal of the print appeared to be lies and propaganda, which made James' blood boil. Even though the South had given up lots in terms of men, material, and territory, in no damn way were they whipped yet. James trembled with resentment at what he read and was greatly anguished by the way his neighbors and one time friends had been so quick to turn against his father.

Unable to do more than sit, wait, and read, time once again stood still for James. The night of May twenty-first was the night his father finally arrived. Jim Wilson's delay had been caused by some really hot action the General had been involved in. Ironically, not with the enemy. Actually, Forrest had been shot. One of his own subordinates had committed the crime. Forrest was one tough son-of-a-bitch, and he managed to stab his assailant mortally after being wounded himself.

The General had come down really hard on a young lieutenant who had neglected serious duties in a previous engagement. The young man could not handle the coarse nature of his commander, thus the shooting. Within two days of receiving the knife wound, the lieutenant died, mortally regretful of his action.

Forrest had promptly moved further South in order to recover in safer territory and Jim Wilson had gone with him, in order to discuss future war needs during the General's down time. Forrest was alive and well and still as active as anyone in his command, giving the wound very little attention. Wilson had just finished telling his story to Duckworth when James walked into the hall to see his father for the first time in almost two years.

Chapter 5
Reaquaintance/Respite

After the many months of guessing and wondering about each other's whereabouts and health, at first neither Wilson was able to move upon seeing the other. After a few seconds, which seemed like hours, the older spoke.

"Is it really you, James? I can't believe what I'm seeing. Duckworth, dammit!"

Before he could finish, he was wrapped in his son's arms and pulled onto the floor. They then stood and began to dance around the room. The Colonel, as was becoming quite common, again had that funny looking walrus type grin on his face.

The Wilsons were completely exhausted after a few turns around the room. They ended up wrestling themselves onto the floor again, talking and questioning each other at the same time.

Where have you been these last few days?" young James asked.

"Where have you been the last few years?" retorted his father.

Once again, James recounted the story of his wounding at Sharpsburg, his recovery, and the journey home.

"There's only one way you could have made it through all that alive! Luck! And, I'm sure glad you got here before it ran out," his father surmised.

"Pa, I've got to agree with you there. Even the war department went to the point of sending you a letter, which I was lucky enough to intercept before you could receive it, informing you of my brave actions and subsequent death at Antietam."

Jim Wilson had noticed James' limp as he moved about the room telling his story.

"I will never march off to war again," he pledged, carefully planning his oath as he spoke.

"Nope," the older Wilson agreed. "I need you to help me here on the farm. With your wounds and my work behind the scenes, we have contributed as much as anyone could ever ask. With your help here, we can do even more."

At first there was no answer. James could only hang his head in silence. He had hoped not to have to face this issue so soon. He knew exactly how his father felt and harbored the same thoughts both before and after discovering his father's operation.

"When I was laying near the Antietam expecting any damn minute to die, I realized how proud I was of what I had done. Now I feel the same pride for you. We've made a damn great effort. To continue might be pressing our luck a little too far.

"Still, somehow, we've gotta do more. From Richmond to here, I saw lots of people who had absolutely nothing. They were going on just the same. I have to go on also. I simply cannot quit. Something inside that I can't control won't allow me to quit..not for you or even for the first woman I ever have felt love for, and that's a subject I'd rather deal with later."

His father then knew that they were through. There was no use trying to change a Wilson's mind.

After dinner that night, James and his dad took a long walk around their home. It was a very quiet and awkward time. At times neither could express himself, so they walked in silence with the only noise being the sound of their bootheels biting the floor.

Jim Wilson was eager to learn all about Camille and the Johnsons. He asked as many questions as he thought James could answer. James tried to tell his father as much as he could.

However, he found there was a great deal that he just didn't know himself about his thoughts and feelings.

"I really don't know what it is. I've never experienced love before, so I don't know for sure. I am sure that all I have to do is see that beautiful face in my mind, and I'm ready to hurry north again, with or without General Lee," he confided. "I guess that's the way you felt about my mother."

"Yes, I remember the feeling well. So well that, even now, I can't dwell on it too long without getting choked up. But, Camille and your mother sound very much alike. As a matter of fact, it sounds like you are as brow beaten as I was," Jim laughed.

"Naw," said James. "She's a good one though. As beautiful as the Confederate flag flapping in the breeze. Her voice was as relaxing as Taps played after a hard day's march."

"It sounds like you're under a double spell, one for a woman and one for a war," Jim joked and eased up quickly, "Don't let it eat your insides out, this double fixation. Fight or don't fight. Stay here with me or head back north with your heart, but either way, make a decision and stick with it or you'll go crazy second guessing yourself."

For two months or so, James remained around the house helping out wherever he could while trying to set his mind straight on one course or the other. During that time, he did not hear or see a single Yankee. That was a good feeling.

After two years of seeing the blue bastards at the end of his rifle and seeing himself at the end of their rifles, he welcomed the reprieve. He also did not see any of his family's old friends from before the war. That was really strange to him. In some cases, he knew about sons in the army who had not been seen or heard from by their family's in many months, some even years. However, given the current state of affairs, he certainly couldn't go calling on anyone for he would most likely be turned in to the Federals by the first people he saw. His knowledge which might have helped others stayed within him. His neighbors' hatred of a situation they could not understand had cost them information about those they loved.

The farm was run just like it looked, immaculately and exactly. Jim Wilson was an excellent administrator. He was hard working and meticulous to a fault. The farm was a personification of the man, methodical and precise. With everything running so smoothly, there was really precious little for James to do to keep himself occupied.

By sleeping normal hours and eating three regular meals a day, James gained to one hundred eighty pounds in weight. It was a damn good thing that he wasn't going back to the infantry, because he certainly wasn't at fighting trim.

There was some excitement on the Fourth of July. A few of the boys in blue got drunk and started shooting their guns on Columbia Pike, right in front of the Wilson house. It was more than they could handle, seeing this rebel family untouched by the war. Initially, the gunfire scared all hell out of James, but he soon realized the significance of what day it was. The elder Wilson thought James looked quite the fool hiding under the bed in his room. He explained that the Feds didn't know that James was home and probably wouldn't care if they found out.

"A few of the boys who were in the Twentieth with you are back," he said, "I don't believe they've had any trouble from the Yanks in charge. I've even seen them on the streets in town.

"It's a damn shame but three out of four of them are missing at least one limb. You'd probably be better off here at home."

James nodded. "By the way," Jim began, "I had a talk with Granger the other day. He has a really bad attitude about the South. If we weren't doing for him what he thinks we are, we would be in a real fix ourselves. Probably as bad as the others. For them, things can get much worse."

James turned the conversation to his departure. He knew Forrest was still somewhere in Northern Alabama and Lee, they had heard, was once again headed north. James' father wanted to know to which his son would become attached.

"Hell," answered James, "Nobody seems to know for sure where the Army of Northern Virginia is anyway, even though they are in good hands. Wherever they are, it would be too damn hard for me to find them.

"I guess I'll stay as close to home as possible and try to join up with Forrest."

"That might be pushing your luck just a bit," interrupted his father. "There is no harder fighter than Forrest. He'll be in the thick of the fight until the very end unless they kill him first. Every boy in blue is longing for the privilege of performing the deed. Think about it, son."

"I have thought about it and I want to contribute, but, stay as close to home as possible. I'm not in any hurry to go right off. I figure I've still got some downtime coming to me before jumping right back into the fray."

The thought of his son re-entering the fight caused Jim Wilson to feel ill inside. He began to pale and to lose equilibrium. Having turned fifty that year, time was catching up with him faster than he realized. Before the teetering Wilson fell, James was able to catch his father. He then helped him onto a couch, and called for Mai and Jacob to help.

"I may be staying longer than either of us ever thought," James whispered.

"Don't worry. I've seen Doctor Clancy," his dad admitted. "This is only from lack of sleep or some other such triviality."

"I got dizzy once before after a week with Bedford and went to ole Clancy. He told me it was just fatigue, dammit. It's funny, he doesn't know the truth about my activities. Get out of my way so I can get up."

James' father was pulling himself off the sofa when Mai crashed through the door screaming.

"Wut's wrong, wut happened?" she lamented.

"Pa's had a second dizzy spell, if he's told us about them all," James said. "But don't worry, he'll be alright."

"Huh," sighed the large matron of the Wilson farm, "He be awright, win he stop actin like he yo age stid uv his own."

Jim Wilson was raising his hand by then, but, it didn't stop her.

"Doc Clancy doan know how much he do. He doan know de real trufe. I do. I seen him wuk day n' night. I ain't no doctah, but, I knows his haht is sick an has been since y' lef heah. Since y' been back, it probly cited him too much. Wut Missa Jim need to do now is res. He needs to res mo dan he do all de time," she prescribed.

Raising his voice, Jim Wilson spoke with authority. "Mai, I hope you will bring my dinner to my room. James, we'll have to finish our talk tomorrow. She's right on at least one count. I need a bit of rest. Believe me, son, I understand your feelings about joining the General. It's really the only way to do it."

As James' father headed to his bed for the night, James embraced him realizing the fragility of life even away from the battlefield. His hug exuded great gratitude and undying love.

James was up late that night as he attempted to get his mind straight. It was a task he had attempted several times before in the past months. He wasn't certain of how to feel or what to do.

The next day, July 5, 1863 news reached Franklin about the double tragedies of Gettysburg and Vicksburg. The shock was all encompassing. Lee was defeated with better than 15,000 casualties while Vicksburg, Mississippi was captured with its full garrison of 20,000 plus troops who surrendered. The Confederacy's most formidable army was defeated in combat and its only link with the West was severed.

The small community suffered extreme depression over the news. The division of General George Pickett had nearly ceased to exist. They did not know it then, but General George Meade had replaced Joe Hooker as the commander of the largest army in the land, The Army of the Potomac. Meade, was a strong defensive fighter who took few chances and was not known for bragging about how he was gonna whip all hell out of the South, as had other commanders. Unfortunately for the South, he was the type of man the Federals needed. A number of gallant Confederate field officers had been killed including two of Pickett's brigade commanders, Armistead and Garnett.

Except for the many Yankees in the area, Franklin became very quiet and sullen little town. It was also demoralizing that the defeats occurred around July 4th, of all days. Soon the feeling turned to depression. With all their efforts underground, the Wilsons, most particularly, felt the sting. James' father needed the support of the community and his friends for the losses greatly pained him. Instead of talking with others about the defeat, he had to pretend to revel in victory. More than ever, he wanted to disclose his true position, to someone. He knew only Confederate military successes would allow that and the latest news pushed his going public even further away.

The situation continued to deteriorate. Duckworth reported that Bragg was slowly being maneuvered out of the state, making Forrest that much harder to find.

On the ninth morning of the month, James approached his father who was at his desk doctoring Yankee numbers.

"Do you think we can endure as a nation with the things that have happened?" he asked.

Slowly, deliberately, his father lay down his pencil and raised his head. He looked at his son for just a few seconds, deep in thought.

"I would imagine," he began, "that the last week has probably nailed the coffin shut. As the optimistic Duckworth has said many times, 'miracles happen', but, I'm afraid I don't share his optimism."

For the first time since his return home, James saw a sign of old age in his father's face. His gaunt expression was etched onto his pale skin which hung beneath sunken, red eyes. His voice, however, remained strong.

"I know that there are many who will not give up until they are killed. Forrest, for instance, I feel quite sure, will become even more intense now. He probably thinks that he has to make up for the reversals. He'll keep on."

"Well, I guess it's time I went to find our old friend," James replied. "I've rested long enough. Maybe too damn long. I'm worried about your health and the safety of everyone here once the Feds figure out what's been going on with their ordinance system. After being away from ya'll so long, it's real hard to leave again."

Jim Wilson also felt the fear of becoming exposed and shared his son's concern about his failing health. He tried not to let on.

"I'm not that sick. I work hard for a man my age. Maybe a little too hard at times. I've made all the necessary plans and arrangements to refugee everyone and everything that is movable to the deep South at the slightest hint of being discovered.

"As a matter of fact, I hope to be long gone from this area several days before the Yankees begin to grasp the situation. On the way out we are going to distribute all extra provisions and supplies to as many families as possible, who live in this general area. I won't be leaving here known by my friends as a traitor to the South. Don't worry. I have the utmost faith we will be together again. Being with Forrest, you will be closer to home and more likely to visit."

On the fifteenth of July, after an emotional good-bye, James headed south in hopes of joining up with Bedford Forrest within the week.

Chapter 6
Return to Active Duty

Mid July 1863 was a very busy time for the Federals in middle Tennessee. All units were gearing up for a big offensive to try to wrest Chattanooga and vicinity from the Confederates. The initial thrust took the Yankees straight south from Nashville through Franklin, to the Tennessee state line which bounded Alabama. The build up forced James to the woods and footpaths, allowing only night travelling. Middle Tennessee is a beautiful place and James enjoyed the scenery.

The area of valleys, pastures, and rolling hills was covered with lush foliage and timber stands similar to Winstead Hill at home. Night travel also afforded him the opportunity to scout the Yankees during the day. He knew what he saw would be valuable information to both Forrest and Bragg as soon as either could be located.

During a three day period, he counted thirty-seven regimental flags of all arms. As he figured it, some 25,0000 to 30,000 of the enemy must have passed under his watchful eye. The masses heightened his anxiety and turned a would-be leisurely trip into a headlong rush. Someone in a position of authority needed to be informed about what was headed their way.

Nine days after leaving Franklin, James arrived in Tuscumbia, Alabama. From locals he found that Forrest had headed east just the day before. Forrest had not wanted to go, but Bragg had fallen back all the way to Chattanooga. Forrest had followed suit in order to avoid becoming isolated and cut off by a force ten times his own strength.

On the twenty fifth, James started east, hoping someone would sit still long enough for him to catch up. Even with his savvy and cool, James didn't like his position somewhere between two antagonistic armies.

Travelling light and fast, James hit Chattanooga on a hot and humid Sunday morning, August first, 1863. The town was not much more than many rows of dirty shanties. The military presence caused his heart to jump into his throat. To the southwest, Lookout Mountain bristled with cannon and infantry. Even further to the south, Missionary Ridge looked like a reflection of the former eminence. The town itself, meant nothing, but the location was a strategic center of rail and communications. Loss of the town meant ultimate loss of the Tennessee River and the last semblance of Confederate control in the state.

Confederate grey and butternut were everywhere in the small city. It had been months since James had seen as much southern military hardware in one place. At least 50,000 troops occupied the town and surrounding heights. They were mean and hungry for a fight. Most were damn tired of retreating. James overheard some Texans on the street talking about the coming fight. They vowed that they had taken their last step away from the enemy and that Longstreet, of all people, and his entire corps from the Army of Northern Virginia, was headed west to help in the inevitable battle.

Longstreet's addition would swell the ranks to some 65,000 to 70,000 men spoiling for a fight. Apparently, the Yanks must have also suffered terribly at Gettysburg, otherwise, things would not have slowed enough in the east for Lee to dispatch his favorite and strongest corps to another sector of the war.

James asked everyone he could about the whereabouts of N.B. Forrest. For several days, he was unable to uncover any information to help him. Finally, one of Joe Wheeler's troopers told him that he heard that Forrest was stationed at Kingston, Tennessee, somewhere between Knoxville and Chattanooga. That seemed logical. In his quest, he had travelled due south, then east. Why not head north and probably, then back west. He figured he just might end up back at home if he travelled long enough.

It had been four, almost five years since James had seen the General. Despite the time between visits, he recognized him right off. He was the most impressive and commanding physical presence James had ever seen. He demanded respect and attention from all. His hair was combed straight back from his forehead with a part in the middle and a grey streak running right above his left temple. The streak resembled lightning on a dark night. His cool blue eyes were lively and animated, leading his mind through a maze and toward his ultimate goal of success. His chin was strong, even though covered by close cropped whiskers that also revealed some grey.

At fifty-three years old, Nathan Bedford Forrest still represented to James and many other Southerners, the most fearsome of all warriors. If Bobby Lee was the Saint of the South, surely Forrest was his enforcer. The man actually scared all hell out of James, as he did almost everyone else he came in contact with.

Overcoming his personal anxiety, James walked right up to the table where the giant labored on the endless mounds of paper that accompanied all positions of leadership in the army. He was much better with a sword than with a quill. Wilson saluted and began reacquainting himself with his pre-war friend. Without looking up from his papers, Forrest growled.

"I don't have time to fool with you, dammit, unless you can take care of these damn papers." He noticed James began to stammer and seemed to enjoy the discomfort he was causing. The General continued.

"If you want to enlist, see Colonel Duckworth. If you want to complain about the viddles, forget it," the General demanded. "What in hell took you so damn long to get here?"

Forrest yelled and Duckworth, who was standing right behind the General's tent getting his jollies at James' expense, appeared. As the Colonel rounded the corner James realized the joke. Forrest rose and extended his hand.

"I'm glad to have any Wilson named James, who just happens to live in Franklin, ride with me," he offered. Through Duckworth, the General had already known of James' intention to "jine" the cavalry.

After several minutes of hearty welcomes and reminiscing, James was dismissed to the care of his new friend, Duckworth. The Colonel informed James that he would be part of the Seventh Tennessee cavalry. The Seventh was Forrest's personal escort. The new trooper was issued a strong bay gelding, boots, sabre, two Colt pistols, and a repeating rifle, all branded or stamped "U.S." James assumed that his weaponry was compliments of his father's efforts.

Most of the men of the Seventh had been recruited from the Madison county area, which made James a total stranger. Duckworth assured him that they all knew his father, and they had been alerted to his coming. Accordingly, there were several stops for introductions on the way to James' campsite. The boys were easy to get to know, taking to him right off.

One in particular, T.A. "Top" Reid, offered to have James share his fire. Top had been transferred to Forrest from the infantry and had just recently arrived himself. He too had been put in the saddle because of wounds he received as a foot soldier. Top had been shot in the left arm and hand, which then lacked two fingers.

"I can ride with the reins in my mouth when I have to shoot or use my blade. I grew up on the backside of a horse, so, I got no problem riding. The last time we were near your daddy's place in force, I took out two Yankees before they even knew I'd pulled the trigger," he boasted. "I heard you was missin' a coupla toes, yourself."

"So?" James asked.

"Us misfits need to hang together. If I ever need a coupla fingers, I'll give a yell. If you ever need the use of my toes, you do likewise."

It amazed James to see how a man, on the one hand, could be so hard and tough, while on the other, could be as amicable and easy going as Top was. In Top, James knew that he had made a friend for life.

Because of James' limp and raw look, most in the Seventh thought he was much older than they were and held him in high esteem. Many could not understand why James, like Top, had come back to the fight. They soon found out. The more time they spent together, the more they found out about the new arrival's determination.

By the middle of August, Colonel Duckworth had appointed both James and Top as his orderlies. They became known as "Duckworth's pet cripples." Again the Colonel knew what he was doing. The pair proved their merit. Their assignment brought with it promotions to lieutenant and greater risks in any fighting that might occur. They didn't have to wait long.

On August sixteenth, the Federals attacked a regiment on outpost duty at Sparta. The regimental commander reported that the Yanks were soon moving in earnest. Within the day, orders were sent north to General Buckner who was commanding a division of infantry in the vicinity of Knoxville, directing him to head south immediately. He needed to have his forces close to Bragg before a general engagement began.

In an attempt to help screen Buckner's move, Forrest's command was shifted on the twenty-fourth to Loudon, Tennessee. With pressure mounting from the north as Burnside struck out of Knoxville, the west from Rosecrans, and the south from Thomas and McCook, who had crossed over to the south side of the Tennessee River, Forrest's strength was increased by the addition of a brigade under John Pegram and a large number of the fabled John Morgan's men.

Morgan's troopers had recently returned south after an ill-fated northern raid in which their leader had been captured and imprisoned. They had a damn good reputation. Forrest's command was grateful for their arrival.

By September first, Bragg had decided to let Chattanooga go and headed for Rome. He must have figured that Thomas and McCook were headed in that direction to cut him off from that major industrial city. Forrest followed suit, but in a boil. He could not imagine giving up Tennessee without a fight. The man seemed to be everywhere at all times. James and Top tried hard to keep up, but it was damn hard work.

Forrest's troopers were ordered to hook up with Joe Wheeler somewhere southwest of Chattanooga so that they could lead the army to Rome. As much as he hated retreat, the General found hope in continued Yankee bungling. Rosecrans had achieved his goal of outflanking Bragg, but at a tremendous cost. Thomas and McCook had gotten around Bragg and were thirty miles from each other and an equal distance from Chattanooga, which was their base and the location of Crittendon's third Union corps.

Forrest recognized the situation for what it was. Bragg's army was within fifteen miles of both Thomas and McCook. Because of superior Confederate manpower, Bragg had the opportunity to crush one and then the other in detail before turning north to finish the job by defeating Crittendon at Chattanooga. It was obvious that Forrest was up for the fight. His body language suggested something big was coming. Confederate inactivity prevailed through the tenth of the month as Forrest tried desperately and unsuccessfully to convince his superiors that he could destroy at least a third of the Federal army with prompt and decisive action.

After waiting for a positive response to his urgent requests, Forrest, on the eleventh, turned on McCook at Ringold and smashed the Union right flank. Only vastly diverging numbers kept Forrest from accomplishing with only cavalry what he had requested a whole corps for from his superiors. Of course, the General was hotly engaged personally often during the day.

Forrest was slightly wounded when he and ten of his escort were surprised by about a hundred Yankees. True to the General's style, he ordered a charge which James and company could hardly believe. Also just as true to form, the aggressive show of force convinced the Federals that more Rebs must have been around, and the Yanks ran. Unfortunately, before they made their escape, one nicked the gallant commander in his right arm. He barely noticed. James rode into the fight with his reins in his mouth while firing both Colt pistols. After emptying both guns, James dropped them to the ground and pulled his carbine from its sheath and shot a young Yankee lieutenant in the face. Fragments of his skull flew through the air onto the troops retreating behind him.

After Forrest taught the Yankees the error of their ways on the eleventh, they immediately began to consolidate their scattered forces in the Chickamauga Valley. The General was on fire. The Yanks had enough time to recognize the error and concentrate their forces before the Confederate high command could mobilize. The opportunity, like so many before it, disappeared before it could be exploited. Everybody in the army knew what was happening except their commander.

For the next several days, as the Federals concentrated, Forrest assailed their left flank. Once again, on the fourteenth, he demonstrated his incredible cunning and daring. The Confederate General, Duckworth and a hand full of other men, including James and Top, came upon a full regiment of Yankee infantry. The Yanks were laying around camp sleeping and playing cards with their guns stacked. They had no idea that any Rebs were anywhere close.

The Federals were isolated with the nearest supporting unit five long miles away. Greatly outnumbered, Forrest quietly divided his men, about seventy-five total, into three groups. Included in his group were Duckworth, James, and Top who circled three miles to the Federal rear while the other two stationed themselves in front and on the eastern flank. After everyone had time to get set, Forrest rode right into the middle of the Yankee camp. The General's movement was the signal for the others to advance, and the Feds were hit on three sides simultaneously by what appeared to be superior forces. Most didn't have time to go for their guns. They arose and stood with their hands held high. Some escaped while sixty or seventy were shot trying to resist the inevitable. Approximately five hundred men were captured, and more importantly so were that number of repeating rifles which were immediately distributed throughout the division.

The total loss to the Confederacy as a result of the sortie was only ten men wounded. Forrest's courage and instinct was contagious and infected his men. They felt that they could whip anybody, anywhere and consequently did.

Even during the intense action in which James was almost routinely involved, he could not keep his mind from torturing his heart with thoughts of Camille. It had been over six months since he had seen her face or touched her beautiful body. The passing of time had neither lessened his desire nor quieted the anxiety of separation. The inability to write or communicate in any other way only intensified his pain.

No one in his company, including Top, knew what made James tick. They only knew that when it came to combat and killing, there was only one man better. That man served as their General. By mid September 1863, Forrest had killed at least thirty men in combat personally. James had been in camp only two months and already had seventeen killings to his credit. Top and the rest of the regiment feared James' recklessness would lead to his demise. Death was not seen as a threat to James, merely a distraction for the despair that devoured him.

On the eighteenth, Forrest was strengthened again by the return of the rest of Pegram's troops. In a bold show of force, Forrest and 10,000 troopers crossed over to the west bank of the Chickamauga Creek, expecting every step to be hotly contested. Rather, they found empty entrenchments. Much to the surprise of the Confederate Army, the Yankees had shifted to the Northeast, positioned squarely on Forrest's right flank. The Federal commander in the area was George Thomas who, unlike Braxton Bragg, intended to take full advantage of his new-found opportunity, striking hard at the men in grey. The force of his attack sent Forrest and the Confederates reeling back to their own fortifications. The battle of Chickamauga had begun.

Forrest's horsemen fought on foot in infantryman-like fashion. The intensity of the struggle was immeasurable. There were two full divisions of Yankee infantry with both artillery and cavalry support attacking the Confederate right flank. Smoke filled the air amidst threatening Rebel yells and cries of agony from the wounded of both sides.

On three occasions, Forrest sent James to the Confederate hierarchy for meaningful infantry support which could tip the balance to the South's favor. James' efforts to convince his superiors of his comrade's opportunity fell on deaf ears. Bragg had decided the night before that he was going to attack the

Yankee right flank with his left. The weakness in Bragg's plan was that the Yankees beat him to the punch, hitting his weakened right flank before he could commit his own troops.

What ate at Forrest the most was having to fight a defensive contest because of tactical bungling. With as little as one brigade of infantry, the General knew that he could have become the aggressor. Around midday, D.H. Hill and Leonidas Polk convinced Bragg to return Walker's infantry division to Forrest's sector.

By the time of Walker's arrival, James had been back on the firing line a good two hours. Once again the wizard spun his magic. His men, though outnumbered better than two to one, were well situated, holding a strongly entrenched line. They were not advancing, as Forrest would have liked; however, they were certainly not giving up any ground. The Yanks were very aggressive with three regiments of fresh reinforcements. The word "retreat" was not found in the vocabulary of General Forrest. His soldiers very grudgingly released any piece of ground to which they laid claim.

James and Top usually fought side by side, with the exception of when one of them was sent on an errand for the General or Colonel Duckworth. Their riflery abilities were among the best in the Southern Army and they worked out a system whereby they could deliver a continuous fire. The system was very simple as long as neither missed their mark. Between them, they had two repeaters and four Colts. One man shot while the other maintained a constantly loaded weapon. Therefore, the shooter was never found with an empty chamber. They would not fire unless the Yankees made a run at the Southern line. They allowed many Federal soldiers an unexpected introduction to their Maker.

Since many Georgians were fighting very near their own homes they fought with greater courage and intensity, enabling the line to begin to progress forward. One brigade from Arkansas and one from Mississippi joined and two Federal lines were overrun immediately. Within the second line were found large quantities of weapons and munitions discarded by the Yankees as they fled for their lives. James and Top came upon several crates of Spencer rifles and cartridges. The weaponry and its compliment were greatly needed.

Forrest's command formed a new line on the Yankees' deserted second line. From reconnaissance reports, he learned that any forward movement from that point would expose his troops to potential destruction. The scouts had spotted a Federal Corps strongly entrenched on Forrest's front and as well his flank. Fortunately the Union General Thomas did not know how few men had taken his second line of works.

Forrest was up for the fight and refused to give ground. He wasn't able to drive a whole corps from his front, however. Consequently, he set about strengthening his position in preparation of moving whenever and wherever he could.

By late afternoon, while the whole command awaited some word from headquarters, all firing had stopped. With the exception of the distant sound of artillery way off to the South, it was quiet. The line being stretched to the northeast in response to Federal movements in that direction was composed of the meanest, dirtiest bunch of Rebs known to man. Forrest asked to be instructed as to how to coordinate his movements with those of the other units along the entire Confederate line. No word came.

Forrest waited for the sun to set, then rode to Bragg's headquarters to get instructions for the morrow and to demand explanations for the total lack of communications. His meeting with Bragg proved most unsatisfactory. The goliathian figure stormed angrily away. With each step he insulted Bragg with profanity. After several steps his profane vocabulary was exhausted and he invented new curse words. His words were more offensive than the conventional language which he had exhausted. One positive event evolved from the General's short trip.

On his way out, he had met James Longstreet, who informed him that 15,000 of the South's finest had arrived from Virginia. A smile creased Forrest's face as he left Longstreet. He foresaw the merit of this hardened fighter from the East.

James and Top were emotionally and physically drained by

the end of the day's fighting. It was September 19, the day before James would enter his twenty-first year. Top noticed that James had received a slight wound above his left ear and informed James of his wound. He had so much adrenaline flowing during the fight, he had not felt it when it had happened. After the firing stopped, the wound became painful. He felt as if he had been hit in the head with an axe. Top cleaned and dressed the gash as best he could. They then prepared themselves to wait for dawn and a renewal of the ballistic exchanges. They had a strange feeling of exhilaration which made them actually look forward to the next day's battle.

James built a fire while they chewed on hardtack. For the first time since they met, he opened his heart to Top. They talked for most of the night.

"I'll be twenty-one tomorrow," he related, "If I live. But if I don't, I want you to contact a man named Reuben Johnson, who lives right outside Frederick, Maryland. Let him know the circumstances of my death.

"Don't worry about my dad or anyone else. He'll find out through the normal, official channels. Johnson has a daughter, Camille, and I don't want her to find out from anyone but her father. They got me back on my feet after I had my ass blown half off at Antietam."

Top agreed to the conditions presented to him by James. The exhaustion of the day's physical efforts, coupled with James' head wound put Top in a listening mood. There was much to hear.

"I know this sounds silly," James went on," but, I guess I'm in love with her. My insides are screaming for this hell to end so I can go to her. But, my head, oh my damned old head, just won't let me walk away. No matter how I try, I can't find a way to reconcile my feelings.

"I hate to burden you with this kind of shit at a time like this, but, I had to tell you in case I catch one. Even if I live, I don't know if I'll be able to talk this way again, so, I better babble on now."

"I didn't know her name, but, the Colonel told me of your

lady. I've been waiting to hear it from you. Dammit, you picked one hell of a time to confide in me,"Top answered. "Duckworth wanted me to look after you, ha, ha. That's one damn hard thing to do, what with the way you've been fighting. You're just a regular killing machine. And look who's looking after who. If you weren't so good at war, I'd probably be dead. You know, my friend J.W., that I'll do what you want when the time comes. Get some rest so you can be ready tomorrow when the Yanks come to call."

As Top began to ease back into the bedroll, James asked with a perplexed look on his face, "What's this J.W. bullshit?"

"Well, J.W., for some days now, I've been trying to figure a name for you a little more descriptive than just plain 'James' ". And I guess I have just done it. I didn't even think it up, it just slipped out. But, from now on, to me anyway, you'll be 'JW'."

While the two slept, the army was divided into two wings - the left commanded by Longstreet and the right, including N.B. Forrest and company, by Polk. Under Forrest was his Tennessee unit, Walker's Georgia group and the boys from Mississippi and Alabama, as well as Armstrong's cavalry, which totalled over 17,000 troops.

The next morning, September 20, 1863, the Confederates advanced all along the line. Being on the extreme Confederate right Forrest encountered reinforcements arriving from Chattanooga in route to general Thomas. Forrest's troopers hit them with a vengeance. Except for the horse holders and some orderlies, the whole command which including James and Top, fought on foot. In their desperation, they overran position after position.

This day saw terrific fighting. Every inch of ground gained was bloody and costly in the extreme. The command resembled a dirty, sweaty mob. The roar of noise was as loud and constant as at Antietam. By mid afternoon, the Confederate right had stalled. Forrest had no idea that he was advancing against a full 35,000 Yankees. He and his men fought like savages against the superior force. They were unaware that their advance had been stopped merely because of a Yankee blunder.

Erroneous reports to Rosecrans made him believe that the main Confederate thrust was being directed at his left. A whole Federal division, which had been pulled out of the center of the line to shore up the staggering left under the weight of Forrest's hard driven soldiers, had not been replaced by any other unit. Stewart's Tennesseans and Hood's Texans from Longstreet's corps rushed into the inviting gap. The grey columns turned right, viciously hitting the Federals in flank. Forrest and the rest of Polk's gallant right continued to pound the Yankee left. Simultaneously, the remainder of Longstreet's Virginians were smashing into the Union right, keeping any help from being sent from that sector to plug the gigantic gap which existed in the center. With the exception of George Thomas, who held off Forrest with a tenacity which would earn him the nickname "The Rock of Chickamauga," the Union army was routed and the run for Chattanooga began. Rosencrans, commanding General of the Federal army, was swept from the field by his own panic stricken troops.

James couldn't imagine a better day on which to turn twenty-one. He had participated in the greatest, most resounding Confederate victory since The Army of Northern Virginia whipped John Pope at Manassas the previous year. He had survived the conflict unscathed. Top had not been so fortunate. He was standing next to both Forrest and Colonel Duckworth when a Yankee shell exploded less than twenty yards away. Neither of his superiors were even scratched, but he took a number of pieces of shrapnel right in the chest. He was sent to the rear with Forrest's personal surgeon. If he lived, he was headed home for good. There seemed to be little hope that he would survive. Top's luck had bottomed out and they called the chaplain to read to young Reid from the Good Book.

That stubborn George Thomas had saved the Federal Army from complete annihilation, holding off the pressure the Confederates mounted against him. At night fall, even the indefatigable Thomas had to retire in order to cover the retreating masses of his bewildered army.

Forrest was different. He was not fatigued in the least. He seemed to be rejuvenated by more intense physical labor and received his respite as a result of activity. The taste of victory livened his spirit and quickened his step. He knew that a defeated and demoralized foe could be more easily crushed when enough pressure was immediately exerted. He wasted no time in heading straight for a gap in Missionary Ridge at Rossville, intent on causing as much trouble as he could for his enemy.

He personally pleaded with Bragg and Polk to hurry forward with as many men as possible. His frustration mounted as Bragg said he would have no part of any hard pressed pursuit at that time. He thought the men of his victorious army were too tired. Winning the field at Chickamauga had cost roughly one-third of the army, and the Commanding General didn't think the survivors should be forced to finish the job. The confidence and momentum the army had achieved with the victory slowly began to slide away. Forrest fumed over the mismanagement of the troops. Without infantry support, there was very little he could accomplish. His efforts turned more to harassment than really hurting the Yankees.

Rosecrans did not intend to give up Chattanooga without another fight. For two entire days after the battle, the Yankee horde was strung out for miles from Chickamauga to Chattanooga almost begging to be driven to hell and back. The common private even understood the circumstances which the Confederate General Bragg could not. Another hard push and everything that had been lost in the last two years could be regained. As subsequent events would prove, Braxton Bragg would never again command respect from the Army of Tennessee.

For the next five days, Forrest's troops fought while the rest of the army recuperated. Bragg eventually replaced Forrest's jaded men with infantry in much greater numbers, but it was too late. By the twenty-fifth, Rosecrans had barricaded himself in Chattanooga with nothing getting in or out.

Longstreet was dispatched with his Virginians to Northeast Tennessee to confront Burnside. In leaving, he vowed he would never serve under Braxton Bragg again. The depleted and equally demoralized Army of Tennessee settled into a siege of Chattanooga. Rumors began to circulate that Ulysses Grant was coming to save the Federals. He was known, even in the Confederacy, as a man who got the job done. All knew that with Grant and reinforcements coming, they could not hold the siege for long. The weight of the North's advantages were coming into play. More resources in men and material would tell the tale if Chattanooga were not quickly forced to capitulate.

Upon leaving the Chattanooga area late in the month of September, James and his company were filled with mixed emotions which represented the full range of pyschological feelings. On one hand, they were elated to be leaving the domain of General Bragg, whom they referred to as "the incompentent." On the other hand, they were overcome with despair, as they knew that their departure, coupled with that of Longstreet, would severely hamper any future Confederate endeavors around the besieged citadel.

If the 15,000 troops of Longstreet and Forrest's men were not replaced by some other body from somewhere, it would only be a matter of time before the Yankees came busting out, recapturing valuable territory and regaining even more valuable momentum.

By the first of October, Forrest's command had fought its way northeast to Loudon, where it had been stationed just one month before. The division consisted of the brigades of Armstrong, Dibrell, Davidson, and Pegram, approximating 6,000 men. It was impossible for the General to rationalize the losses and hardships that the command had endured in the last month, for they had not gained a complete victory. They had fought on an almost daily basis for the last thirty days. Rations for horse and rider were at the starvation level. Rest, recuperation and refitting was absulutely mandatory in order to remain an effective fighting force. Duckworth set about the task of acquiring and distributing forage throughout the command. Small contingents of men were dispatched to various counties in the area to obtain the needed supplies.

Confederate high command incompetency interceded to spoil the positive steps which had been undertaken by the General. Bragg ordered Forrest to relinquish his command to

Joe Wheeler, a cavalry leader of some reknown. Forrest had great respect for General Wheeler, but was not inclined to release his troops. Forrest had raised and equipped his division at his own expense and personal risk as most were taken out from under the noses of the Federal authorities on his last West Tennessee raid.

In order to insure that his feelings were properly communicated through the correct channels, he fired off a crisp letter to Richmond explaining his grievances about the existing situation. The issue was formally closed when Forrest gave the brigades of Davidson and Armstrong to Wheeler for his raid into Middle Tennessee, while he retained command of Pegram's and Dibrell's brigades. Fortunately, the Seventh was part of Dibrell's command, so James stayed with the General.

Both Brigadiers, Armstrong and Davidson, considered the proposed expedition as tickets to disaster. Orders were, however, orders. Therefore, they left for Middle Tennessee. That left Forrest with roughly three thousand troopers who desparately needed to refit. For the first time in the war, he found that he too was human and needed some time to regenerate his energies.

In a matter of days, he secured the necessary provisions for the troops and mounts and made plans for himself to see his wife for the first time in over sixteen months. On the day before the scheduled departure, James decided to pay a visit to headquarters.

James knew there could be no way that he could find relief concerning his anxieties about Camille, but he hoped he could obtain information about either his father or Top. As was usually the case, Forrest was much too busy to give him any personal attention. He found Colonel Duckworth with the General and he was more than willing to see James. Without hesitation, James quizzed the Colonel

"I know that I'm no different than any other man in the command, but I sure would like to find out anything I can about my friend, Top Reid," he explained. "Is there any chance that he might survive?"

Duckworth was visibly worn down. His usual droopy smile was replaced by a frown. The consumate professional, he put on his best airs and answered, "You know; I'm sure, my boy, that we have been swamped by all the administrative details that follow any fight, but, most particularly, a big one like Chickamauga. For as many of our dead for whom we can find any family, we have to contact those families to let them know. We owe them at least that much. For so very many, there is just no one to notify. And the wounded like Top have to be removed to convalesce somewhere in safety.

"If that were not enough, we have to file after action reports with the war department. They will take several weeks to compile and submit. I guess, I've gone the long way around the barn to answer your question, but, I just haven't received any word at all. I would like to know something myself.

"I believe that the surgeons, knowing how important he is to us, would direct me to fill his position permanently if they knew he was not going to be able to return to active duty.

"Until he returns, you'll have to pull double duty, but I'm sure that you will be able to handle it. I suppose you wonder about your father, and I am afraid I have little that I can tell you regarding him either. But, I can tell you that supplies continue to arrive from your farm. That flow would certainly end if there were any problems.

"I assume you wish you had headed West with Joe Wheeler. To be perfectly honest, the General and I discussed it, but you're just too valuable to us here."

One thing James' father had taught him early in life was that if you expect too much, you are bound to be disappointed, but if you expect but little, sometimes, you will be pleasantly surprised. He had not expected to discover anything about either his friend or his family, so he left his meeting feeling upbeat. Both must be alive or there would be some word to the contrary.

After Forrest had been gone five days, word reached Duckworth, the commander in Forrest's absence, that the remainder of the division had been transfered to General Wheeler. The

Colonel immediately wired Forrest to return and the General was quick to answer the call. Upon his arrival on October ten, after reading his new orders, he went into such a rage that no one could approach him. He tore his headquarters tent to the ground before setting out for General Bragg's headquarters at Missionary Ridge. Everyone in camp believed that he was going on a mission to kill. After the General had been gone ten minutes, the Colonel summoned James and they left camp in hopes of cooling the General's temper before something rash occurred. They could not catch up with Forrest until two days and ninety miles later. Unfortunately, Forrest's temper had not cooled by the time he got to Bragg.

James and Duckworth arrived just as Forrest was leaving Bragg's tent. To their relief, they found that Braxton Bragg was alive though mentally maimed as a result of the verbal attack he had endured from Forrest. There were others present to relate to them what had been done and said when Forrest rudely interrupted his departmental commander. Upon seeing General Forrest approaching, General Bragg had risen from his work, and extended his hand in greeting. Forrest completely ignored the attempted salutation and lashed out at Bragg.

"You are the most incompetent son-of-a-bitch I have ever known. I organized this body of troops at my own expense and labor, just like the one before it, only to have it taken away and wasted. That won't happen again, for I will never serve under you again in any capacity. You know damn well, that, if I wanted to ride my troops right out of this army no one, except maybe Pat Cleburne, could stop us. If you ever interfere with me again, it will be at the peril of your life!"

It was an error in judgement on Braxton Bragg's part to try to take anything from Nathan Bedford Forrest. Forrest left the camp as quickly as he had arrived. Not knowing what kind of reaction would be forthcoming from Bragg, the Colonel and James waited for several minutes in the camp. When they saw that no reprisal was contemplated, they headed for their own camp. About three miles out, they found their chief waiting for them. His only words concerning the unpleasantries were, "Mark my words, the man is a coward. He will never mention this to anyone." Not another word was spoken between the three men for the whole trip back to their camp.

Subsequent to Forrest's verbal explosion, he and three hundred of his previous command were transferred to the newly created department of West Tennessee and Northern Mississippi. At its core were one hundred hand-picked men from the Seventh Tennessee, including its Colonel and James. At worst, they would probably pass within a few miles of Frankin, as the General would surely reach into the Middle Tennessee area on his way west in an effort to recruit and gather men and horses. They knew of one sure source of horse flesh. Forrest had proposed the move in August. The adoption of his proposal seemed to please him greatly and they looked forward to their new undertaking. James especially awaited the possibility of seeing old, familiar faces, one in particular. This time, he could not help from expecting something good.

Chapter 7
New Domain

By the end of October, Forrest's small band of veterans had traversed a circuitous route of some two hundred miles from East Tennessee south to Dalton, Georgia, then west to Rome, Alabama. They then headed north by west to the Winchester, Tennessee area. Always one step ahead of the game, the General had contacted James' father, through his many scouts in the region, and had arranged to meet him in order to acquire as many fresh mounts and other war materials as Jim could provide. The dilapidated condition of the command was still evident and had even intensified. These hardened veterans really looked like no more than an organized mob of roughians. There were also the new recruits to consider. All that could be obtained was badly needed. Their final destination was Okolona, Mississippi, where they were scheduled to set up shop on November fifteenth. There was little time to spend in the Franklin County area, as the Federals, who were thick as ticks on a dog, would soon discover their presence, and be on their trail.

Fortunately, Jim Wilson was most timely. The entire camp was surprised on the morning of November the first, to see a large herd of healthy horses led into their midst. James was elatedly surprised to see his father and his old and trusted friend, Jacob, at the head. There was great excitement throughout, but nothing could exceed the ecstacy of James, his father and Jacob. After several minutes of laughing, hugging, and tears, Jacob left with the other hands to take care of the stock, while the Wilsons and Colonel Duckworth headed to the

General's tent to discuss the current situation.

The General was not a drinker, but James and his father sipped on some fine brandy, compliments of the Yankee General Granger.

"Jim, I can't begin to thank you for all of your support. You Wilsons have certainly helped me an awful lot," Forrest began. "You've probably heard that your son is quite a soldier. The scuttlebutt around our campfire is that he is the best fighter in the stinkin' regiment. I've seen him in action myself, and I can tell you that he makes me glad that I'm on his side."

"General, we know that the war effort is not going well. I'm concerned that Gordon Granger is possibly getting wise to what's happening back home. It's a gut feeling more than anything, but I've seen some signs. Nothing big, mind you, but some things beginning to change.

"The Yanks are getting bolder, bolder with each passing day. We've even caught one or two sneaking around the farm. Oh, there's always a good explanation, but I don't like the looks of things."

"Well," the General began to respond, but, unabashed, James cut him off.

"Don't go back. Just stay away from there."

"I have to go back, for several reasons," his father argued. "First it's our home. Most of our people are still there. Mai and all her family. If I don't return, the Feds will know for sure that something is wrong."

"Your father's right, James," Forrest offered, "We have to play this thing out or it'll blow up in our faces. Your father is as cool a customer as you are. He'll handle it correctly."

James was crestfallen, but he understood logic when he heard it.

"Trooper Wilson," Forrest commanded, "Take two weeks leave and head back to Franklin with your father to take care of all those Yankees in the event of trouble. The way you fight, I'm sure you can handle just about anything that comes down

Columbia Pike."

Forrest was smiling broadly, which relieved James tremendously.

"Now ya'll get some food and rest and prepare to leave at first light."

"What a great man to serve with," James thought as he and his father left the General's tent.

Around the campfire that night, James told his father about life in the cavalry and his fallen friend, Top Reid. He described Chickamauga and Top's wounding. Trying to hide his anxieties, he did not even mention Camille.

"Any word or news from up North?" his father asked.

"No," James shook his head, "I think about her almost all the time. I think sometimes that I fight harder in an attempt to block her out of my mind."

"Son, please don't get yourself killed over this," his father pleaded. "The only way you will ever see her again is by staying alive. You know she's in good hands. You've told me that her father is a very good and resourceful man. He'll take good care of her."

"I know that Pa, but rationalizing just doesn't ease the pain."

"You'll feel better when we get home in a few days," his father emphasized. "Now, try to get some sleep. We've got to get an early start tomorrow. I've got to see Jacob tonight about preparations for the trip back. I'll see you in the morning."

Jim Wilson eased himself up, leaving the comfort of the warm fire and his son's company and went in search of Jacob. James had the first reasonably good sleep that night that he'd had in many weeks.

Chapter   8
War With Forrest

"I guess we're out of business," Jim Wilson sighed, as he watched the flames leap around the brick structure that used to be his home. The horses stammered and shifted as if they somehow understood that they were witnessing a calamity. James and Jacob could hardly contain themselves.

"We've got to go in," James shouted.

"I be goin, no matta wut," responded Jacob. "All yuh two gots down dere is sum bricks 'n mud. My own blood cud be spilt."

"O.K., you go alone, and on foot. James and I will make our way over to the valley west of Carter's Creek with the rest of the men and wait for you there," the older Wilson ordered. "You be real slick. You can't afford to get caught by the Feds headed home from a southerly direction."

"And, Jacob, for God's sake, find your grandmother first," pleaded James.

"Yuh don has t' wury nun Missa Jim, I knows wut I'se lukin fo, an it hain't no Yankee goods. Bein night 'n all de cumotion, Ise be able t' blin right in. Yuh know's how dem yanks tink 'at we's all luk de same. Dey probly don't eben know I bin gawn. Isa find Mai 'n inny de oders 'at I kin, an meet yuh in de valley 'morra night. I gonna sholey fine de trufe bout wut happen yere. I got no mo t' say. See yuh nex dawk."

Jacob began the long walk down the face of Winstead Hill,

where the small party had first seen the fire's reflection in the clear northern sky. James again scanned the area around Columbia Pike in an attempt to discover if there was any movement on the road headed south looking for them. There was nothing. They were so far away, they could hear only silence from the direction of the fire. Thanks to the brilliance of the flames, they could see many figures moving in and out of the light, apparently trying to extinguish the blaze. Neither James nor his father could understand the situation. If the Yankees had discovered the Wilson's scheme, and had burned the house in retaliation, they would also be on the lookout for Jim Wilson.

"We'll wait here until we can ascertain what's happening down there," Jim Wilson spoke. "No fires or moving around. We can't take a chance on being detected. The Yankees will investigate anything that might seem suspicious." James sensed his father's overwhelming physiological and psychological fatigue, and tried his best to sooth him.

"At least, we are alive. As Jacob just said, 'as long as Mai and the rest of the family are alright, what have we really lost?

"Other than the buildings, nothing was ours to lose. As you told me many times, it had to come to this sooner or later. The Yanks had to catch on sometime. Two years of being a parasite on the Federal war system, the whole time having them believe that you were a contributor to that system is phenomenal.

"Can you count the number of horses, guns, shoes, boots, or food that you furnished to the Confederacy? You might have a record of all that somewhere, if I know you. How much more could anyone person have done under any circumstances?"

"I know all of that," responded his father. "Even though I knew that some day we would all have to leave this place, I was never forced to face up to it 'til now. I'm most worried about our people. What if the Yankees have harmed Mai?

"I don't think I could walk away from that, do you ?"

"No, Pa, I couldn't and wouldn't. If anyone is harmed in any way, someone in blue will pay. I pray to the Lord Almighty that no harm has come to any of our family.

"We are all very tired, and, since we're gonna run a cold camp tonight, let's combine our bedrolls and sleep next to each other. That way we can warm our spirits and our bodies."

Being the first week in November, even sleeping together, the cold was bone chilling during the night. Both Wilsons woke up stiff and chattering, longing for a fire to provide some comfort. The sight below them completely superseded any feelings of physical discomfort. The only thing standing that once was the magnificent Wilson home were two soot covered chimneys facing each other from the east and west ends of the house. The other brick walls had collapsed sometime during the night. Additionally, all the fencing and other out buildings had burned to the ground. The scene was one of complete desolation. The standing chimneys served as the only reminder of the prosperity that had once occupied the grounds. No furnishings had been saved. To their credit, the Federals had done a thorough job.

After several minutes of silent vigil, Jim Wilson began to gather himself and his tack for the short journey to meet Jacob, Mai, and the rest of their people. Scanning the entire area with his binoculars, James saw that there was not a soul on the roads or anywhere around. He could not imagine that the Yankees wouldn't be combing the countryside looking for his father.

"Too many pieces are out of place here. Being with General Forrest these last few months has taught me to look for things that should be, but aren't," James told his father as they walked quietly down Winstead Hill. "And for things that are, but should not be. We should have seen a sea of blue in the last twenty-four hours. We must be careful until we can find out what's happening around here."

James' father smiled and nodded, proud that his son was no longer a boy. The valley was well hidden, surrounded on all three sides by rugged hills that were too steep for anyone to descend. There was a narrow path leading down the face of the most southern hill which could be used, but only by someone who knew the terrain. That path was the only way in or out. Carter's Creek began from a spring that bubbled up from the western boundary and traversed the center of the valley until it went back underground through the northern boundary, coming back up several hundred yards out of the valley to flow into the Harpeth River northeast of the little town. Most of the inhabitants of Franklin didn't even know that the valley existed or of the origin of Carter's Creek. The small hut and corral they had built at the start of the war were still standing, a tribute to it's secrecy. The holding area at the edge of the woods offered ample security for the Wilsons and Samuel and Isaiah, who had accompanied Jim Wilson and Jacob on their trip to Winchester. There they anxiously awaited Jacob's return.

Shortly after nightfall, they saw a group of silhouettes begin the descent into the valley. Remaining cautious, James slipped out of the camp to find out who was headed their way. Within the hour, James returned to report that he had heard Jacob's and Mai's voices distinctly along with several others from the farm. He couldn't get close enough to discern what they were saying, but, he was sure it was them. Shortly thereafter, the group arrived, filled with disbelief.

"Lawd Missa Jim, twerent no Yankees 'at did 'at burnin. It wuz de nabahs!" Mai cried, visibly shaken by the terror of the preceding day!

"Now, you just sit down here and rest," Jim Wilson suggested, concerned about his servant. "I can't believe you even came down here.

"What's come over you, anyway? This is too strenuous for you. You know we would have come for you."

"We had ta, Missa Jim," Jacob interrupted. "She needs t' tell yuh hussef wut happum."

"De udda white folks 'at live neah y' fom is de' wunz 'at lit d' fiah. We's thought dey wuz jes cummin t' pay a long ober du visit. Dey tole weuz all t' git out as quick as we's cud, din out cum de tortches." Mai explained.

"Wait just a minute," Jim Wilson pleaded as he couldn't believe what he was hearing. "You mean it really wasn't the Feds?"

"Now, y' jes seddle down, Mammy," Jacob interjected, "I's

tell de res. She right, Missa.' D' yanks, dey don't know nuttin. Daze de one's who try t' putt it out. I eben tawk t' de udda black foke who cum t' try t' hep us out. Dey say at d' white fokes had a big meetin d' udda night n' decided t' burn yuho out fo heppin d' yanks."

"Hell!" Jim Wilson sighed. "They just didn't know and, now they will probably never know. Are any of our people hurt or killed?"

"No sa, Missa Jim, but dey sho scart. An, d' nabahs, dey will fine out de trufe. Fo dey lef, we tol sum d' udda darkies d' gospel trufe bout yuh."

"But, Jacob, that could endanger the others left behind," James said.

"James," Jacob answered, "De' res already dun headed souff. Bout sunup a Yankee sojer cum t' de place, all upset. He give weuz hosses and a caht sa weuz cud git away. Affa he lef, dey all headed t' Columbya. De Yankees want t' fine Missa Jim fo sho. But, dey tink t' bury him. Dey tink d' udda white fokes dun kilt him."

"Well," Jim Wilson continued, "this is too incredible to fathom. We should have let somebody know. I was so damned stupid."

"No Pa," James offered, "This was really the best way for it to happen. It's a clean break. Nothing to go back to. All of our people are out safe, and the Yankees will not be hot on our trail. Our friends will know sooner or later of their mistake. Now, all you have to do is make your way safely to Columbia with Jacob and the others here to meet the rest. Then, refugee south. I'll strike out to Okolona to meet the General and let him know what has happened.

"In a way, what's occurred here can really be viewed positively. At least we know there's no quit in Franklin. They're still decidedly for the Confederacy."

Jim Wilson had a queer expression on his face. One that his son read immediately.

"Oh, no, Pa, you're not going with me."

"Oh, yes I am. As you said to me several months ago," his father answered, "It's something I have to do. Now that our little ruse is exposed, there's no other path for me to take."

"But, Pa," James was more forceful than his father had ever seen him, "You're just too old for battle or the things I've seen and done."

"Like you, my mind is made up, and that's that," Jim retorted.

"I'm going to protest to the General," James interrupted.

"Forrest and I discussed this many times in the past, knowing that in the real world, this day was coming. He needs every man he can get. As a matter of fact, there's a captaincy waiting for me, probably in the Seventh, with you."

"I can't fight in a war worrying about you all the time," James countered.

Calm and confident, Jim Wilson responded, "Exactly, what do you think I've been doing about you all this time. I'll take care of myself as well as you do yourself. Besides, it will relieve both of our anxieties knowing where each other is. Now we've got to head for Columbia to make the necessary arrangements for Mai and her family to travel to Mobile where they can book passage to California and your aunt. Even without the Yankees combing the area looking for us, we've got no time to waste."

James was dumbfounded, but relented. The next night, they met the rest of their people on the outskirts of Spring Hill where they secured enough mules to carry all of them on to Columbia. Amidst sorrowful goodbyes, they left their people with the needed papers and sufficient money to reach Mobile where highly respected friends of both the Wilsons and the General would secure passage on the first available blockade runner which would take them to the Bahamas. From there they could make their way to California to wait for the two Wilsons to join them.

There was much risk involved in a journey of that length by that large a group of free Negroes; however, it was a risk which had to be taken. The pain of separation caused Jim Wilson too much sorrow for him to say the words he felt, but everyone knew how he cared for he had done all that any man could have done.

His son, however, was a different person. As he hugged Mai and Jacob, the tears flowed freely, something he had told himself many times in the last several months would never happen again. His love flowed just as freely as he feared it might be the last time he ever saw them.

"I never thought I would see this day," he choked, "leaving ya'll in this situation. You've got to stay together and use every precaution. Jacob, you know you're in charge. Take care of Mai and all the rest. I love you all more than I can ever put into words."

"I's take care dese young uns, no matta who yuh putt n'charge. Yo jes take care of y'seffs, an git thru wid dis yere fight quick as y' kin. Weuz be waitin, n' matta how long it take. Yuh wach affa y' daddy n' tink uf us win y' kin. Yo knows weah weuz be. Now, git, fo I side not t' leab," Mai replied.

After their last embraces, the Wilsons mounted to ride for Okolona and Bedford Forrest. The sorrow of departure overwhelmed the two strong men and forced them into silence as they rode southwest.

By the middle of the month, time and distance had removed some of the remorse that the two carried with them. As they crossed into Mississippi on the twentieth, they began to see and hear of the results of General Forrest's activities. From inhabitants along the way they learned that the General had secured at least two thousand recruits and great quantities of provisions in anticipation of a thrust into West Tennessee. The populace had given abundantly, responding to the positive effect the General had on all with whom he came in contact. The departmental commander was Stephen D. Lee, who had offered the General every possible assistance. Through his influence, the war department had promised to forward guns and munitions that could not be obtained elsewhere. Forrest was extremely gratified to serve under a man who fully recognized and appreciated his unique talents. Although Major General Lee was Forrest's superior, he offered to relinquish all control in order to further General Forrest's achievements. He could not, however, cause the ever tardy war department to take his subordinant seriously enough to forward the promised weapons.

By the first of December, all was ready and Forrest could wait no longer. On December second, the entire command, including half without arms of any kind, crossed into West Tennessee. The resourceful Jim Wilson was made a captain of scouts and his son was transferred to the same unit as a lieutenant. Their immediate superior was Brigadier Tyre Bell, who hailed from Jackson and had been sent ahead to that town to spread the word that Forrest was coming. True to his trust, Bell had secured many additional recruits and mounts. The Wilsons and fifty others arrived in the Jackson area on the fifth, and with Bell, set about the task of organizing the new troopers' in preparation to Forrest's arrival on the sixth. Up until the twentieth, the command gathered itself and ample provisions, again with the notable exception of arms.

The Federal departmental commander was Major General Stephen Hulburt. Knowing that he, as did many in the Confederate high command, took the sortie less than seriously, Forrest took enough time to accumulate a herd of cattle and hogs, much needed clothes, and other needs, along with the many recruits who flocked to his banner. There was a general outpouring of help and encouragement from the people of Jackson and Madison County. During the two week stay, there was much gaiety and many balls at which delicacies of all descriptions were heaped on the General's men.

At one such affair, James was astounded to find his friend and comrade, Top Reid. When he walked into the great hall where the banquet was being held, he could hardly believe his eyes. He quickly found that his friend was only a shadow of his former self. Top had to remain seated most all the time. When he stood, he required assistance for he had lost a great deal of weight and was very weak.

Conversation was very laborious as the wounds had severely damaged his lungs to the point that his breathing was extremely shallow. Even so, he demanded as much of James' time as he could.

"I'm so glad you made it out of that last fight, J.W. With me headed to the rear, I had no idea who would take care of you," Top lightly laughed.

"Well," James responded, "I sure didn't do too good a job taking care of you my friend. I'm just damn tickled to see you here. Not hearing anything all this time, I really thought you had gone up for good."

"It'll take more than these holes in my chest to kill me. But, I won't be fighting anymore," Top coughed.

"Don't you worry old pal," James offered, "We'll take care of the Yanks for you. We're here, ain't we? Nobody has ventured out to make us move. You look after the home front and the General and company can handle the war front."

After several hours, Top grew weary at which point a kindly Jackson matron took him under her wing to escort him back to bed and much needed rest. For the second time in the past few weeks, James couldn't stop water from filling his eyes as he watched his friend depart.

On the twenty-third, word reached the General that the Yankee commander in the West, William Sherman, had prodded Hulburt to move. Using all the available men and resources in the area, the Federals planned to encircle and entrap the 5,000 Confederates congregated at Jackson. Moving swiftly, Forrest started his troopers south on December twenty-four. Under the able direction of Tyre Bell, the rest, including the large quantities of provisions followed close behind. The Yankee trap had been sprung without its game. By the first day of 1864, the entire command had safely reached Holly Springs, Mississippi.

For the next three weeks, Forrest reorganized and refitted his 6,100 troopers into brigades and divisions, commanded by Brigadiers Richardson with 1,500 men, McCulloch with 1,600, Bell with 2,000, and Jeff Forrest, the General's brother, with 1,000, with divisional commanders Chalmers and Buford. James and the Seventh, including one hundred handpicked riders led by Jim Wilson, who were the General's escort, were part of Jeff Forrest's elite 1,000 of Chalmer's division.

Forrest held his headquarters at Oxford, constantly on the alert for any Federal move aimed at his discomfiture. He knew that the embarrassment he had caused the Yankees on his last trip north was bound to grate on those in power, who felt the sting of his operations. He operated freely and openly, right under their collective noses, with astute maneuvers and decisively prompt action. As always, the man was ready and looked forward to any contest. He had gone into West Tennessee with barely 1,000 poorly armed and equipped raw troops and emerged with six times that number, loaded with ample provisions of all types, fresh Yankee mounts, and unbounded spirit. While many were still unarmed, he knew full well that as soon as the command came into contact with any Federal force of size, those unarmed would become armed with the finest weapons that Yankee money could buy.

In camp, word reached the General that Sherman had embarked from the Vicksburg area intent on traversing the central part of Mississippi in route to Meridian, the major Confederate manufacturing center in the state.

Through Hulburt, at Memphis, Sherman had instructed General William "Sookey" Smith, to head due south toward a junction of his and Sherman's two bodies of troops at the Mississippi capitol. Forrest had no plans for Bill Sherman, but for Smith, he could hardly wait.

Smith was so timid, that he did not even depart Memphis until the day before he was scheduled to meet Sherman at Meridian. With a body of troops equal to that of Forrest, he delayed until the arrival of a regiment under Colonel Waring, headed south from Paducah. Waring turned out to be the only fighter in the group. The 7,000 Federals arrived at Okolona on the eighteenth, on the way to West Point. From West Point, Forrest decided the Yankees would advance no further. It had deeply bothered him that the enemy columns had invaded his domain and that they had left a path of destruction in their wake. All citizens had suffered at the hands of the vengeful Smith. Retribution was at hand.

After allowing the Federals to penetrate as far as West Point, the General knew that when he hit them, they would be bounded by several swollen streams and rivers that would severely hamper any retrograde movement.

On January 19, Jeff Forrest's boys smashed into the Yankee van. General James Chalmers was in command of both Forrest's and Bell's brigades as the fighting commenced. He had Forrest hit the Federal front while Bell and his troopers headed west to come in on the Yankee's right flank. As the battle was beginning to heat up, General Forrest arrived at the point where General Chalmers was tactically directing the action. As always, he had his one hundred man escort with him. He ordered Captain Wilson to remain several hundred yards to the rear while he and Lieutenant Wilson went toward the sound of the firing to examine the situation.

Forrest was unable to learn anything of consequence from Chalmers and refused to remain uninformed. He then left for the front with James and General Chalmers in tow. Accustomed to his leader's ways, James was undaunted. It was apparent though that Chalmers was dismayed by his superior's action. Although, he was afraid to advance as far forward as Forrest, General Chalmers headed into the fray, expecting any minute to be the recipient of one of the many bullets that were flying about them as the enemy began to take their measure.

As the three were approaching the firing line, a thoroughly demoralized soldier dropped his weapon, turned, and ran straight for the rear. Unfortunately, the path of the poor wretch carried him right toward General Forrest who immediately dismounted, threw his reins to a smiling James, and prepared to receive this bewildered soul. As Chalmers began to protest, Forrest grabbed the fleeing trooper by the neck and vigorously threw him to the ground. Turning this fully grown, but panic stricken man over, the General gave him the most severe and thorough thrashing of his life. He picked the man up by the scruff of his neck, and faced him about.

"You had just as soon return to the fight, for if you ever run again, I promise that you will die in the rear." the General pledged. "The next time, you will not get off so lightly."

The desired effect was achieved and the frightened trooper

straightened himself, grabbed the nearest weapon, and headed back to the fight. He eventually became one of the most able riders in the entire command, serving with distinction until the end of the war.

Soon the concerted efforts of Forrest in front and Bell on the flank caused the Yankees to begin to give ground. As always, looking for any opportunity to strike at a vulnerable spot, and seeing the enemy beginning to retreat, Forrest rode down upon the relenting Federals. Knowing that a demoralized foe offered very little resistance, he disregarded the overwhelming odds faced by his hundred, and cut the Yankee rear into shreds.

By the time the Yankees reached the outskirts of Okolona, all of the General's troopers were mounted and riding hard upon the fleeing foe. With the General, his escort, and those of Chalmers' command who could keep up, chopping at the front and Bell still harassing the flank, the situation became extremely desperate for the Federals. Once through Okolona, the Yanks reached ground suitable for another stand.

They deployed as many stalwarts as could be mustered, and prepared to receive the coming onslaught. Their respite was very short. Forrest was far ahead of a great many of his troops. Unflinching, he gathered his escort around him to offer instructions to prepare to close with the enemy at close range. Sabres and pistols were to be utilized. Against the pleadings of Jim Wilson, he led his body forward to do battle. As they rode into mortal combat with their enemy, the advance elements of McCulloch's brigade came into sight of the fierce fighting that was swirling around their beloved leader. McCulloch immediately signaled the charge. Seeing some of his men wavering from the seemingly overwhelming weight of numbers of the antagonist, he called to his men.

"Do you see your courageous leader surrounded and imperiled? I will go to his aid even if I go alone."

Five hundred stalwart followers slammed into the Federals like a tidal wave. The Yankees were, once again, completely routed. During the height of the struggle, James and Jim Wilson, father and son, had been right beside their General. James had felled one of the foe as the Yank was about to sabre the General from behind. Forrest returned the favor by decapitating a Yankee who was close to clubbing James with the butt of his repeater. The prompt action of McCulloch settled the issue.

As the Federals continued their scamper north from Okolona, they discarded many valuable articles of war and other much needed provisions. One army's trash proved another's treasure and this garbage was most welcome to Forrest's warriors. They also left a number of their wounded who had no chance of escape. One such unfortunate, who was losing an arm to amputation when the Confederates arrived, was disgracefully left by the terrified surgeon with the cutting tool left in the marrow of the bone. Forrest heard the pitiful moans of the soldier and immediately stopped to investigate to see if he could help the deserted soul. There was another side to the General. It did not matter that the wounded man had chosen to wear blue. Seeing the condition in which the surgeon had left his patient, the General put him under the care of his personal physician, Dr. Cowan. After waiting awhile to insure that Cowan was able to tend to the man, Forrest again turned his attention to the wounded soldier's comrades.

The General's brother and Colonel Bell had continued their hard pursuit. At Ivey's Plantation, the Yankees made a stand. With Jeff Forrest now on the right flank, McCulloch on the left, and the General in front, the Yankees again yielded to the tremendous pressure. As the last of the Federals were making their escape, the impetuous Colonel Forrest was killed while in hot pursuit. The death of the General's beloved brother temporarily put a halt to the onslaught. When the news was delivered to General Forrest, the command seemed to sense that it was a time to stop and all pursuit ceased as the General rode far to the flank to his brother's fallen body.

For several moments, the General held his deceased brother in his arms. He then laid the spiritless body upon the ground. Raising himself to his full height and stature, he called for his favorite bugler, Gaus, and ordered the charge. Every man responded to the call with renewed enthusiasm and untempered zeal. Very few could keep up with their leader who was filled with rage from the loss of his sibling. Forrest and his escort, now reduced to sixty, outdistanced all others in the command and hit the fleeing enemy with a force that was unparalleled.

About four miles north of Ivey's Plantation, several hundred Federals under Colonel Waring, formed a rear guard to allow their comrades time to make their escape. It, however, was for naught as Forrest rode right through those brave Yankees, killing many and capturing around one hundred before they could withdraw. The utter exhaustion of his troopers forced Forrest to give up the ghost at that point. In three days of fighting from January twentieth through the twenty-second, his men had inflicted four hundred casualties while incurring only one hundred fifty. The Federal force had been completely routed, returning to its base at Memphis with its tale between its legs. The Confederates' morale was boosted to new heights with its overwhelming success against the Yankee General Smith.

As a fitting reward for services gallantly rendered, the General's command was given a month's rest for much needed rest and recuperation. Chalmers' division, composed almost entirely of men from the deep South, was furloughed en masse. Knowing that these riders and fighters would return to the banners for which they had fought so fiercely in the past within the prescribed thirty days, they were allowed to go to their homes for new horses and clothes. It was hoped they would return with additional recruits. Being mostly from West Tennessee and Kentucky, the division of Abraham Buford was kept in camp in anticipation of yet another raid into West Tennessee. Only the General and his divisional commanders knew of the planned sortie. Rejoicing at the seething and obvious irritability of the Union high command, Forrest had determined early in February to attempt to increase the rancor of Bill Sherman even more by wreaking havoc in the Yankee back yard. He had had his eye on the Federal stronghold, Fort Pillow, for quite some. The capture of the fort would add a substantial feather to his cap.

After a month of reorganization and refitting, Forrest departed his camps on March fifteen destined for his home grounds. With him went the entire division of Buford, the brigades of Thompson and Bell, and the Seventh Tennessee, plus a battalion under Colonel McDonald. His escort, under direct supervision of Jim Wilson, led the advance. With the exception of four or five scouts, who were always deployed two or three miles ahead of the column, the General, accompanied by Captain and Lieutenant Wilson, proceeded the troops on their northern thrust. His escort had become the focal point of almost everyone's attention, both in and out of the command. Every man under the control of "ole Bedford" strove to become part of that elite body. Although the escort was officially part of the Seventh, it was in actuality made up of various appointees from anywhere that the General happened to choose. And his choices were quite selective. Many of the Yankee papers found the need to report on the activities of the General and his escort.

The Wilsons were the best fighters and riders in the unit. Every man added to the body tried to emulate the father and son tandem. It was the most dangerous position to which any trooper could aspire and the most honorable.

The intense activity seemed to rejuvenate Jim Wilson. The worry and anxiety his son had felt for his safety had not dissipated, but James was much more comfortable with his father fighting by his side. Both men constantly looked out for the other and on several occasions, they were there to offer a slash or shot which would prove lifesaving. It seemed they had reversed their roles. Jim acted much more animated and irresponsible in battle than his son. Yet he was into his fifties. He was one of only very few who engaged in combat at that age, besides the General.

James had matured well beyond his years as a result of riding with Forrest. His experiences would prove invaluable to him if he lived through the fight, something that very few, including the General, thought would come to pass. As the troops passed through the most northern boundary of Forrest's domain, the General and the Wilsons engaged in conversation about happier and more secure times in the years gone by.

"I guess we never envisioned how far this fight would take us from those tranquil times that we knew before," the General noted. "When we began freeing our people, I felt that others would follow suit and hold off this fight."

"But, how could they?" Jim Wilson rhetorically rambled. "Agriculture is the South's meal ticket. Very few could make it work without slave labor. As you know, the only way we were able to make it was through damn hard work. Without both James and I doing as much as we did, our little experiment would never have worked."

"But," interrupted Forrest, "It worked, and when this is over, it will work again. Your people will be waiting for you to start again when the war ends. And, that might be sooner than anyone thinks."

Puzzled, James and his father could only exchange glances of surprise at their friend and leader who was showing a prophetic side which the Wilsons did not know existed. There was only one man in the entire command who could call the General by his first name. That man was Jim Wilson.

"Nathan, do you think we are defeated?" he asked.

"Well Jim," his long time friend replied, "Not through lack of effort, mind you, but through lack of power or strength, however you want to call it, and the mismanagement of those few resources that we have had. I'm afraid that the West has been lost through bungling on the part of the Generals in command. I feel absolutely certain that the South cannot fight its way to freedom or that it can exist as an independent state without the West, or at least, control of the Mississippi River, which of course, we don't have."

"Then why do we go on?" James asked.

"Because, Lieutenant, maybe the Yankees will misallocate their resources or bungle their own opportunities. And as you should know yourself, there is a man in the East named Lee, who has worked several miracles in the past. Maybe he can continue his magic until the Federals give up trying to beat him.

"There is the possibility that the Northern people will tire of the fighting and dying, and just let us go from sheer exhaustion of effort. All of those factors are long shots, but there is one other variable that drives this man. My home is threatened. I would rather be dead than have my home and family subjugated. So, I will keep killing Yankees until they kill me or give up trying to do so."

Forrest usually let his actions do the talking for him, and his speech included more words than he had spoken to anyone in quite some time. Reflecting on the General's wisdom, the three settled into the quiet of the ride north.

Five days later the 2,800 men reached Jackson, where they stayed only enough time to rest for a few hours before proceeding on to Trenton. At Trenton on the twenty-second, Forrest detached Colonel Duckworth and the Seventh, without the General's escort, to head north to invest the garrison at Union City. With the remaining 2,200 troopers, the General headed due west toward Fort Pillow. Under the ruse of the name of Forrest, Duckworth was successful in his quest of Union City. Colonel Hawkins, the Union City commander, had been duped by Forrest or his subordinates before. After seizing all supplies and paroling the captured men, Duckworth headed southwest for a junction with the General.

By April ninth, Forrest had consolidated his scattered commands from Northern Mississippi, West Tennessee and Kentucky, where General Buford had ventured in an attempt to capture the important supply depot at Paducah. Buford and his troopers, who had covered the most territory in the shortest time, were left in the Covington/Brownsville area to guard for any Yankee interference while the rest, including Chalmers' division travelled due west to Fort Pillow.

On the twelfth day of April, the command, consisting of some 3,000 troopers arrived at Fort Pillow. The fort rested high upon a bluff over the Mississippi River and was surrounded on its eastern, northern, and southern sides by eight to ten foot embankments with an outer line of entrenchments in front of each. Blood ran high throughout the command as many of the forts garrison were known Tories who had committed varied atrocities on the families of many of the men of Forrest's command. The commander of the fort, Colonel Booth, was killed in early skirmishing as he attempted to reconnoiter

Forrest's advance positions. Command of the 575 man garrison had evolved to Major Bradford who had declined the grey General's offer of surrender.

Bradford was given a second chance to capitulate after seeing the General himself. After refusing to surrender and thereby save his command, he issued great quantities of liquor to his mixed troops of black and white men. The desired effect was to strengthen the resolve of his men in the coming fight. The effect achieved was the overwhelming disaster of those souls who fought on after reasonable resistance had proved fruitless. After his second rebuke at the hands of Major Bradford, Forrest and James personally patrolled the grounds to insure that his troops would take the most direct routes of attack, insuring as little loss of life as possible. In the fort, many defenders took note of him and his aide, and began to fire at the pair. They also shouted, and made abusive gestures. This did not go unnoticed by the men about to assault the fortress.

Upon returning to his own lines, the General ordered his bugler to sound the charge. The battle plans were perfectly executed as the leading squadrons jumped into the deep ditches in front of the entrenchments to help propel those that followed into the fort. The fighting was extremely fierce as the assaulting forces closed with those defending the garrison. The drunken state of the Federals did not hold them in good stead as they were vigorously attacked from three sides at once by an overwhelming force. When the General saw his troops enter the perimeter of the fort, he rode to the scene to put a stop to the one sided fighting.

After gaining the inside of the garrison, the Confederates saw that the Federal flag had not been removed from its flagstaff, which indicated that the garrison had not given up. Bradford was immediately taken prisoner and the flag hauled down in the hope of saving as many of the forts combatants as possible.

Many of the intoxicated black troops continued to resist, however, resulting in the death of many more men than would otherwise have occurred. All total, nearly three hundred troops were killed in the struggle. In its propaganda, the North labelled the disaster a massacre and branded the General and his command as murderers. In reality, Forrest had done everything in his power to minimize the killing even as the garrison attempted to receive relief during a truce by having a nearby gunboat come to its rescue. Had the use of whiskey not been so liberal, the death toll would have been much smaller.

With Forrest's successes in West Tennessee so impressive, Grant and Sherman became intolerant toward their General Hulburt and replaced him with Cadwallader Washburne. Washburne brought in Sam Sturgis to pursue Forrest in the hope of eliminating him before he could get out of the state. The Yankees were too late in their movements. By May third, Forrest had arrived at Tupelo, Mississippi with 5,000 men and many and varied supplies of meat, lead, and leather all of which were badly needed provisions. Safely out of Forrest's range, Sturgis reported to his commanders that he was too late to bag his game. On the sixth of May, the Congress of the Confederate states officially thanked General Forrest and his whole command for their valuable service.

May, 1864, seemed an eternity from the spring of insurmountable confidence back in '61. The three years seemed more like three decades to the majority of those who fought for Southern independence. Even those who were lucky enough to serve under a winner such as Robert Lee or Nathan Forrest were in bad condition. Jim and James Wilson served as perfect examples of the wearing down process that constant fighting could impose. Like most of the men in Forrest's outfit, the two had grown long unkempt beards to protect their faces from constant exposure and their hair grew to the length of the soldier's shoulders.

Although there were no regulation kepis to be had from any source, they were not wanted, as all found out early that the best screen for the eyes was a soft felt type hat that would slouch in front. Everything else that was not of U.S. issue was homespun and usually torn and tattered. With their long hair hanging out of the sides of their hats beyond the beginning of their beards and the front of their head gear partially covering their eyes, the Wilsons looked like a pair of twin devils. The amount of war devices that they carried on themselves and their mounts consisted of two navy Colts strapped to their sides, a carbine or repeater occupying a saddle sheath on both sides of their horse, and a regulation U.S. sabre.

Riding with the General could not relieve the acute problem of constantly dwindling supplies of horse flesh. The Northern Mississippi and West Tennessee regions had been thoroughly picked over by the ebb and flow of contending armies for a full two years of war. The South did not have a holding farm such as the Wilson's from which fresh mounts could be obtained from the Yankees without having to fight for them. Forrest provided well for his troops in spite of the fact that supplies were falling on all of the other fronts. Everyone usually received a fresh mount after every encounter with the Federals, now; however, they were forced to last until the next such clash. Serving with Bedford Forrest was damn hard work for man and beast.

The worn down and dilapidated condition of the command caused the General a great deal of concern about the near term effectiveness of his force. He knew that he had to give his men down time to rest and time to forget fighting. As though Providence were looking down on him, the Federals again dispatched his most recent victim to other duties in another department. They then replaced the defeated commander with another more favored and confident General who seemed better suited to the task of bringing in Forrest's hair. Fortunately for Forrest, it took his new adversary, Sam Sturgis, almost a full month to surround himself with the near 9,000 infantry and cavalry to complete the work which was left undone in the prior attempt to capture the General. The month's respite was not as much as Forrest wanted, but it was greatly welcomed.

Chapter 9
Depression

No one on either side in either theater of the war, could envision that the final phase of the war was beginning in May of 1864. Acting upon the advice of Bill Sherman, Ulysses Grant had devised a grand strategy for prosecuting the war by utilizing a scorched earth policy toward noncombatants. He could not perceive of the extreme catalytic effect of those policies once he had begun. Robert E. Lee and those gallant souls of the Army of Northern Virginia had no idea that the campaign they were about to begin in the Wilderness was to be their last meaningful attempt at offensive warfare.

The Army of Tennessee over in North Georgia was at its maximum strength and spirit for the long series of battles that would culminate in the loss of Atlanta to Sherman's Yankee host. Even though the odds were very long, Bobby Lee could have held out much longer in the trenches at Petersburg had Atlanta not fallen. Both of the principle armies of the South lived to fight again after their exertion at The Wilderness and Atlanta, but as a great deal less than the mighty fighting forces they once had been.

Nathan Bedford Forrest was a realist. Like Grant and Sherman, he could read the handwriting on the wall. If Sherman could be stopped, Atlanta might be saved and allowed to continue to produce the vast quantities of munitions and other war materials. Then, conceivably, the South could prolong the fight indefinitely until the North grew utterly tired of the struggle. Many on both sides of the Mason Dixon Line referred to Forrest simply as "The Wizard of the Saddle," but it took no wizard to see that the only way that Bill Sherman was going to be stopped, short of serious tactical blunder on his part, was to cut off his flow of supplies. An army on the move, like a snake, crawls on its belly. Besides the immense quantities of agricultural supplies, there was no strategic value in the Northern Mississippi area for the Union armies.

Grant and Sherman clearly recognized the potential negative implications of a "Devil" like Forrest let loose to roam freely in North Georgia and Middle Tennessee to disrupt the flow of ordinance and communications from the invading Yankee army to its bases of supply. Although both of these most powerful Yankee generals had not felt the sting of defeat in this conflict, the possibility of such could prove to be a bitter taste. They were willing to accept that fate on a front rather than their own if it would insure that N.B. Forrest were kept busy so as not to interfere with their grand strategy for ending the war. Indeed, they counted on the consistent ineptness of the Confederate high command to continue. Their perception and strategy would, of course, prove to be correct.

Forrest realized early the game that was being played, and he pleaded with his superiors through every possible channel to give him the authority to perform contrary to Yankee wishes. He knew that he could defeat any forces that were organized and sent against him. His scouts notified him of any force venturing into his department, risking sure defeat at his hands. True to form, Jefferson Davis and his advisor, Braxton Bragg, refused to release the General from his own department, and thus insured the success of Bill Sherman in his efforts against Joe Johnston.

Like his men, the General was weary, tired of body and spirit from almost constant fighting and continual contact with the enemy. His will was inwardly shaken by his failure to convince the Confederate powers that be to loose him on Sherman's supply route. Consequently, he petitioned his immediate commander, Stephen Lee, for a rest. As evidence of his broken down physical condition, his body had broken out in boils. There is some question as to how effective the General would have been operating in Sherman's rear at this particular time given his overall condition. But, there is little doubt that a great deal of his physical problems were due to psychological and emotional fatigue from energies wasted in dealing with his superiors. In any event, he was immediately granted a personal furlough.

James spent the time of respite writing letters which he feared in his heart would never be delivered or received. There were no mails transferred from the South to the North except in extreme cases, and only by those who were close to enemy lines and at a heavy cost. Even under those conditions, there were no assurances of delivery. But, he wrote them and dutifully posted them with his own postmaster all the same. The commissary agent of the Seventh, who took and delivered whatever pieces of mail were circulated, only smiled whenever James arrived at the little table of an office to post his supposed communications. Like many of the men in the General's command, James and his father were allowed to come and go in camp as they pleased during their brief interlude from fighting. It was hoped that those troopers who lived in the region would be able to secure fresh mounts from their families and friends and maybe enlist some new recruits. Being the harvesting season, many left with every intention of returning after helping their families yield their crops to carry themselves and the army through another several months of hostilities.

Traveling freely through the region, the Wilsons saw much of what the struggle had exacted from its' inhabitants. Many had given more than one son or brother or father to the precious cause. Farms which were once beautiful and well kept were in many cases deserted serving as ghostly monuments to the conflict of man. The bitterness derived from the tremendous toll required of the people coupled with his longing yet unfulfilled need for Camille, made James become more and more despondent with each new day.

This newly acquired physical freedom allowed Camille's absence to dominate his thoughts which should have been reserved for battle. The great thing about battle was that it took all his attention to keep up with his General and stay alive. The fighting also allowed him to vent his frustrations on a body of men with whom he had every legal and moral right to attempt to destroy in mortal conflict. In battle, he had a very definite advantage over his adversaries. He could see it plainly in the eyes of those he had killed or maimed. While they were afraid of death, he was not. Compared to the despair of living, death would be a relief. Until some Yankee got lucky or he became sloppy, James Wilson would remain the most proficient and fanatical killer in all of Forrest's command.

It was not long before Sam Sturgis began to move, necessitating Forrest's early return and subsequent recall of all furloughed troopers. The corps was put in readiness under the able leadership of its divisional commanders Chalmers and Buford to await the coming struggle with the advancing Federals. Sturgis left Memphis on June 1, with 3,300 cavalry under Ben Grierson, 4,800 infantry under Colonel McMillin, and twenty-two guns serviced by 400 artillerymen. Also included was a wagon train of two hundred fifty in number loaded with provisions of all types including forage for the many animals in the column. The region in which they were traveling had given all that it could to the many who had exacted its yield. Forrest waited with approximately the same number of troops as his newest adversary. Chalmers' division consisted of three brigades of 4,800 men while Buford commanded 4,000 troopers in his two brigades. Also available for the fight were sixteen pieces of artillery ably manned by two hundred fifty hardened veterans.

The considerable pomp associated with Sturgis' departure from Memphis was soon washed away with the torrential rains of the season which slowed the progress of his little army to a crawl. To make matters worse, when it wasn't raining, the temperature and humidity reached killing levels producing heat strokes for many of the men and animals. Most of the forage which had been brought along was consumed in the first several days of the march and the barren nature of the terrain precluded replacement. By the ninth day of the month, the force had only reached a point nine miles north of the hamlet of Brice's Crossroads.

Ever resourceful, Forrest welcomed the weather as an ally. Knowing that the combination of rain, heat, and humidity would ruin the Federal infantry for a fight, he waited at the crossroads for the cavalry which was moving several miles in front of its nearest support. The General skillfully deployed his men with Chalmers' division hidden in a dense woods to the west while Buford took about half of his men to the eastern flank. He sent Barteau's second Tennessee circling far to the east with orders to hit the Yankees in the rear as soon as he heard the sounds of battle. He kept his escort and the remainder of the Seventh with him to attack the Union front. As usual, the signal for the general advance was to be the sound of his personal attack on the Yankee force.

As the already played out Federal offensive stumbled toward the crossroads, the General saw his opportunity. With three hundred fifty hale and hearty followers, he smashed into the dilapidated blue column. Before the Yanks were able to form to receive the charge, Forrest had closed in with pistols and sabers. James and Jim Wilson were right by the General's side, slashing and shooting at anything in blue. Totally ignoring their flanks, the Yankees concentrated all of their available force toward the front to deal with Forrest and his small contingent. Like clockwork, Buford and Chalmers, upon hearing the firing, immediately hit the Union flanks. Dead tired and assaulted on three sides, the Federals had no choice but to retreat. As they attempted to retire in an orderly manner, Barteau's Tennesseans screamed into their rear, hitting their wagon train and creating panic. The Federal cavalry was routed in a disorderly fashion, losing its entire train and twelve guns.

Several miles north, the fleeing horsemen took refuge behind a hastily formed line of dog tired infantry. At that point, realizing that the overwhelming fatigue that gripped his men would make continued assaults fruitless, Forrest called a halt to the pursuit. Still, as Sturgis limped back toward his base, the General nipped at the Federal's heals with as many of his men as could carry on. The continued harassment allowed the Confederates to capture the remaining artillery pieces of the enemy along with a grand total of 2,000 prisoners and all two hundred fifty of the Yankee's wagons and teams. A mere 3,000 of the Federals made it back to Memphis on the fourteenth. The embarrassment of the Union expedition caused the dismissal of Sam Sturgis, who was replaced by yet another Smith, A.J., who vowed to have the hair of N.B. Forrest. Sherman had made his desire known in several communiques to his subordinates expressing a deep longing to see Forrest's scalp.

There was very little to rejoice about in the Confederacy in mid June 1864. Robert E. Lee and the Army of Northern Virginia were engaged in a struggle for their survival with Ulysses S. Grant and the Northern Army of the Potomac. Mile by tactical mile, Bill Sherman was eating up North Georgia clay in route to capturing the second most inhabited city in the South, Atlanta. Both The Army of Northern Virginia and The Army of Tennessee were still full of fight, but the weight of numbers was squarely against them. Only Nathan Forrest and his resounding successes in Northern Mississippi served to lift the spirits of a populace which was becoming increasingly dispirited with each passing day.

Even so, Jefferson Davis and his advisors, primarily Braxton Bragg, would not give up their antiquated departmental style of prosecuting the war. Both of the major Southern armies would be well served by giving up North Mississippi to the Yankees by sending Forrest into Middle Tennessee or even North Georgia to wreck Sherman's communications. As circumstances prevailed, there was nothing left for Forrest to do but fight where he was.

And, fight he would. His newest antagonist was A.J. "Baldy" Smith. Smith left LaGrange, in southwestern Tennessee on July 5, ostensibly headed to wherever Forrest was. He had with him, two infantry divisions of 11,000 men commanded by Mower, one cavalry division of 3,200 troopers under Grierson, and a Negro brigade commanded by Colonel Moore. There was also an artillery battalion of twenty-four guns manned by five hundred gunners. Generals Buford and Chalmers were waiting for the Union advance at Pontotoc with 7,000 Confederate cavalry. Before colliding with these able and daring disciples of Forrest, Smith turned east and headed for Tupelo, which Grierson was able to capture on the thirteenth.

On July thirteen, a series of events occurred which proved disastrous for Forrest's command. With the state threatened on several sides, the departmental commander Stephen Lee, who had previously endeavored to assist Forrest in every way possible, took personal command of the situation in the hope of striking a decisive blow quickly. This would allow him to turn his attention to other beleaguered areas of his department. Lee proved to be quite inferior to Forrest in every aspect of military science.

After relinquishing command of his troops, the General and the most trusted member of his escort, Jim Wilson, went on a personal reconnaissance of the Yankee positions which ultimately took them up and into the Federal camp. By adeptly avoiding the Yankee pickets on the way in and by pretending that they were high ranking Union officers on the way out, they were able to successfully ascertain that the Yankee position was much too strong for the morrows coming assaults. But, General Lee could not be dissuaded in his desire to make short work of the contemplated action. He believed that Forrest's men were capable of herculean accomplishments, which they might have been had their own General been leading them. As it was, most knew that the sure and steady guiding hand of Forrest had not been in favor of the attack which they were ordered to carry forth on a numerically superior foe.

Early on the fourteenth, 5,000 Confederates viciously attacked 14,000 Yankees posted behind strong earthworks and were just as viciously repulsed. There was no movement to gain the Federal rear or flank as would surely have been tried had Forrest been in charge. The grounds over which the Confederates were so severely whipped were what was once the small town of Harrisburg. The city was by then a totally deserted area. It was just as well for fully twenty percent of the Confederates engaged were listed as casualties. It was not a sublime moment of Southern pride. What had been a very agreeable relationship between Forrest and Lee soured badly as Forrest never forgave the impetuousness of his commander which cost him the useless loss of so many valuable fighters.

Regardless of the outcome of the fight, Smith was so intimidated by the gallant assaults of the Southern soldiers, that he began to withdraw immediately after breaking off from the engagement. With his temper up, Forrest determined to sting his adversary all he could before the Yankee column could reach safety at Memphis. As he followed on the heels of the retreating Federals, the General was shot in the foot. He was forced to dismount by his personal physician, Dr. Cowan, who noticed a trail of blood behind the General. The wound proved to be less than serious, but very painful. Forrest took to a buggy from where he reorganized the command in preparation for the return of Smith or whoever the Yankees might send after him next. Although Baldy Smith had not bagged Forrest, he could legitimately claim to have wounded the "devil," something that none of his predecessors had been able to accomplish. That alone kept him in his job, at least for a while.

As he was with the General everywhere he went, James had not taken part in any of the fighting that later came to be known as the Battle of Harrisburg until about the time that the General had been wounded. That was the first actual fighting that Forrest, personally, had performed on that field. Like all the other members of the General's escort who had to watch the slaughter of so many good men, James seethed with bitterness over the sight unfolding before him. He knew that with the type of rashness displayed at Harrisburg, the South could not continue to hold out much longer. There were no replacements for the many who had perished on that bloody field.

Following the excitement and the carnage of each battle, thoughts of Camille pelted James' mind. Time normally eases such emotions, but he could not let go. The only time the haunting ceased was in the heat of the fight. Day or night, unless he was at play at his deadly game, her face was always there. He knew it would take death to set him free. If that was the answer, he would continue to give it every chance to liberate him.

Everyone around him knew that James was possessed by a spirit that was bigger than he was. He had begun to withdraw from everyone except the General. James' father was certain that his son had a wish to die. He never laughed or joked with any of the other men in the ranks. He only wanted to kill! Jim Wilson had talked to Forrest about his son. The General had, unfortunately, dismissed the situation in his usual strong manner. Apparently, the two were too much alike. The General had the same substance running through his veins. The difference was that the aggressiveness of Forrest was not linked to a woman. Jim Wilson pleaded with Forrest to give his son some time away from the fighting. But James was far too valuable to the General for him to consider letting James go. Whatever plagued young Wilson would just have to work itself out. His father prayed that somehow, it would.

Chapter 10
The Dream/War's End

James rounded the bend on Columbia Pike about one hundred yards south of where his house had once stood. He was riding hard and fast. About fifteen Federals were right on his butt. He knew that his father and Camille would be waiting at old man Griffin's shack at Thompson Station somewhere around midnight if he could only make it that far. First, he had to get off the main highway and into the surrounding woods to shake that squad of Yankees who seemed real intent on putting a bullet in his back.

They had spotted him as he was passing the Carter place on his way out of town. Being so close to sundown, he hoped to catch the Yanks between patrols, making his exit out the main highway relatively safe. He could not have been more wrong. The incoming unit had spotted him immediately. Even so, he wasn't worried. If caught, they probably wouldn't hang him for he was as fully uniformed as any Rebel could be at that stage of the war. He hoped that they could not come close to catching him. This was his country; he knew every inch like he knew his own mind. He could even hide from his own family, and often did in happier days, in this neck of the woods.

The only real risk was that one of those boys in blue would get off a lucky shot, for they could not possibly see him in the twilight of a mid September day in Middle Tennessee. As he passed beyond the shadows of Winstead Hill, he turned hard to the right, going up a path that he did not see, but knew from experience was there to take him out of harms way. As silly as it seemed, he relished the excitement of the chase.

It was August second and the command had been widely scattered so that both men and animals could recuperate and refit more easily. Although Forrest had not whipped "Baldy" Smith, he had shocked the son-of-a-bitch badly enough so that he was not going to crowd the General too much anytime soon. Forrest wanted the Wilsons to return home to scout the area, so he said, and see if there were any available men who might have left other commands in the field, but would now agree to serve with him.

Forrest had acquired hundreds of recruits in just such a fashion. This practice intensified his strained relationship with the war deparment. Its incompetence, in his opinion, was ludicrous in regard to the transfer of men. According to the war department, these recruits were deserters who should have been either prosecuted or returned to their original units. However, these deserters were willing to fight for the cause, but only in their own area and under leadership of their choosing.

The thought of returning home had been just the tonic that James had needed to snap him out of the mean and sullen mood that had gripped him for the last several months. What he wasn't told until several hours out of camp was that his dad had received word from the Carters that they were keeping a young woman from Maryland in their house. A woman named Johnson. Seeing the dark side of his most favorite and trusted scout growing more and more with each passing day, the General finally acquiesced to James' father. He ordered them both home in the hopes that both would return with the proper frame of mind required to help him achieve positive results.

Having heard reports of Miss Johnson's arrival and having noted that all James' interest was in killing and his determination to die, Forrest felt the move was better for all concerned. James' dad had warned him many times on the trip that the communiqué he had received from Fountain Carter could have very easily been erroneous or even misunderstood by his son Todd, who had delivered it on his way to the Army of Tennessee after a short visit with his family.

To the great delight of James, the message was correct. As

before, when he had returned to a home that still stood and thrived, he could hardly contain himself sitting on Winstead with his dad, waiting for the proper time to approach the Carter dwelling. It was the eighth day of August at about two in the morning when they awakened the Carters and discovered that Camille was truly there. He could hardly believe his eyes. The war had yielded so many unbelievable things to him since he had been that young buck back in '61. He had lived through Antietam, his father's work done for Forrest and the Confederacy, and the burning of his home by his neighbors.

Fountain Carter had been a willing participant in the burning of the Wilson home. It had taken several weeks for the truth of Jim Wilson's operation to circulate throughout the Franklin community. Fountain Carter, feeling the guilt of the unnecessary destruction, was willing to keep a Yankee girl in his home in order for her to await the return of his neighbor and her lover, James Wilson. The most amazing and incredible fact of the whole thing was that the beautiful young woman could not only love James, but could find a way to be with him in the midst of the hideous inferno called war. The gods of love and war worked in mysterious ways.

Jim and James Wilson had spent most of August and the first few days of September stealthily scouring the country side by day for any potential recruits, and by night seeing and visiting old friends and neighbors within the relative safety of the Carter's home. The townsfolk had come either individually or in a group no larger than three to express their appreciation to the Wilsons for their contributions to the war effort. Most were outwardly ashamed of their part in the burning of the Wilson homestead.

There was no animosity in these meetings, however. The realization of the community that the Wilsons had not turned on their neighbors was satisfaction enough for father and son. And there was, of course, some precious time for James and Camille to be together.

James desperately longed to be out of the fight, and Camille was equally as desperate to return with him to his safe haven in Bedford Forrest's domain. Both knew that neither goal could be obtained in the real world of hatred and killing. They spent many nights together in the shanty in the hidden valley. Their passion and loving was many times stronger than it had ever been before. After so many months apart, they fully realized that they could become parted forever in just the blink of an eye.

They talked little as words could not express the depth of their feelings. When they spoke, it was not as before. James had come to see things about himself that he could never share with any person, even the woman he loved. Yet, he opened up to her as much as he could. One night as August turned into September, they lay under a bed of bright Tennessee stars and a gigantic full moon as James tried to relate to that wonderful creature which he held in his arms, how his senses had changed with the passing of time while in war.

"I don't imagine I've spoken a complete sentence to anyone, including my father, in several months. After seeing our house burned to the ground and learning it was done by people we loved, I was so confused. Especially without you here to help me through it with that damn hard headed common sense of yours, all I could focus on was fighting and killing," James explained. "I ride with the most fearsome leader and outfit of soldiers that either side can muster. The only way I can see of ending this horrible nightmare is by either killing as many of the enemy as I can or getting killed trying. The General, he's as feared as any one man, anywhere, but he also has a good heart. I saw him personally save a wounded Yank at Brice's Crossroads in a situation where I would have shot the poor bastard, thinking I was putting him out of his misery. I've lost all focus on what's right and wrong."

"James, my darling, I know you've changed," Camille whispered. "I could see it the first time you walked through the Carter's door. Your appearance is almost like that of an animal. And your eyes, they don't shine like they used to. But you're in a war, not a picnic dammit."

He had never heard her use any kind of curse word before. So, he was shocked to hear it now.

She continued, "I don't love you one bit less for what you've become. If you had not changed the way you have, you just might be dead right now instead of making love to me. We got all the news up in Maryland about your beloved leader General Forrest and his many successes. Every time the news got around that he had whipped another one of our cocky generals, I thanked God for the achievement. You see, something in my heart told me that you had not only made it safely home, something that we never knew for sure, but that you were riding with this giant of a man.

"If serving with the most feared man in your precious Confederacy and turning into a hardened killer is what it takes for you to be safe and alive, so be it. If that's what keeps you alive so that I can be with you, then I know that you must return to him. I also know that I can not go back with you, but that you are going to leave me as your wife and with your child growing inside of me."

James stammered, "Wait, what, are you crazy or something? We can't."

Before he could finish, she cut him off. "Unless you don't love me anymore, we will marry before you leave to rejoin your comrades. I'm already pregnant. I saw a local doctor two days ago and he confirmed what I already knew."

"You know I still love you," he sighed. "You know I want you to be my wife. But, ah, what if I don't come back? What would you do? How would you take care of the two of you?"

"I'm very disappointed in you," she retorted angrily. "How do you think I got here? Have you seen my father anywhere around here? No, you have not. I came alone with his blessing, because he knew I was coming anyway. I took real good care of myself. You're not the only one that this war has forced to change. Besides that, this thing can't go on much longer, and you will return. I know that as sure as I knew that I would find you alive when I got here.

"If," Camille choked on the words, "If you don't live through this thing, my father is waiting for my return to him. Of course he has no idea I'll be bringing a baby with me.

"After I gave Mr. Carter the letter of introduction from my

father, he has treated me like one of his own. So, I know that if I want, I can just as easily stay here among your people, and be welcome."

As she finished, having spoken more forcibly than usual, Camille sank to the ground, exhausted.

James could barely control his emotions as he reached her side. "You should have told me before now that you were carrying our child."

"Why? she looked deeply into his eyes, "would it have mattered?"

"I guess not," he whispered.

The next day, they were married near midnight in Fountain Carter's parlor. Jim Wilson served as best man while one of the Carter daughters, Varina, was the maid of honor. There were no guests, but they didn't need any.

Having lost the Yankee patrol which had been on his heels previously in the dense forests at the base of Winstead Hill, James was looking forward to meeting his father and new bride for a short good-bye before the two men began the long and dangerous trip back to Bedford Forrest. They had been moderately successful in their effort to find recruits. Almost three hundred were going to rendezvous with them near the Tennessee River below Florence.

His feelings of elation quickly gave way to despair as the searing pain in the back of his head brought him back into focus with the real world. His father was looking down at him with an obvious look of relief.

"Don't try to move just yet, son," he said. "That bullet you took just grazed the side of your head. You've been unconscious now for four days."

As James began to question where he was and what had happened to him, he remembered the shouts and firing by the Yankees in the streets of Memphis as the General's raiding party made its way out of the city. It was August twenty-fifth, and he was in a home in Okolona, safe behind Confederate lines. Awakening to what he did after the dream he'd had,

James could only moan. In his delirium, he had called Camille's name on numerous occasions. What a wonderful time it had been. Now he was forced into reality. He was so physically weak from the wound and so emotionally drained from the trauma of his return to the war which he had left only in his mind, that he was unable to get out of bed for several days. Finally, on the third of September, after the news of the fall of Atlanta had reached him, he forced himself to get up so as to find his weapons. If it was killing the world wanted from him, he had plenty to give.

For three weeks, James was allowed the luxury of recovering from the head wound he had received on Forrest's Memphis raid. The entire camp reveled in the joy of riding, almost completely undetected, right into the headquarter's city of the whole Union department of the West. The Yankees felt so secure with Smith out on the trail of General Forrest that they did not feel compelled to adequately guard their base. The Federal Generals, Washburne, Hulburt, and Buckland were hurried out of their respective bedrooms without even enough time to dress.

What Forrest had achieved as a tactician against the over-whelming weight of numbers attested to his military brilliance. His forces had been too greatly depleted to meet the needs of other parts of his department. It seemed impossible that this devastated group could have accomplished the Memphis raid during which they were able to capture the uniform of the semi naked, fleeing General Hulburt. Against great odds, the South had prevailed.

For James these three weeks did not bring happiness. The realization that his wedding had been a dream made him even more depressed than before. As was always the case when a chance of battle presented itself, he had looked forward to the raid on the extreme Yankee rear. He had counted on doing great damage to the Federals in their most vulnerable spot. He had succeeded in killing several of the enemy. It did not bother him so much that he had been wounded. But, the dream had seemed so very real. The fact that it wasn't, took him farther away from the real world around him. Physically, he healed. But nothing would heal his emotions. For the last week of his convalescence, he sat with all his weapons close at hand, cleaning and cleaning again until blade and barrel sparkled with shine. Not a word from his mouth fell upon the ears of another soul.

Although the Confederacy had played right into Sherman's hand by removing Johnston and replacing him with John Hood, the high command in Richmond finally called for Forrest to move his troops into Middle Tennessee in the second week of September to operate on the Yankee line of communication. Hood and the Army of Tennessee had already been thoroughly whipped in combat by Sherman's blue horde and Forrest's command had been drastically reduced. The Southern move was the epitome of "too little, too late." Still, most of the men who remained with the General to begin the campaign into Tennessee, were from the Volunteer State and were damn glad to be headed home to fight for a change. Although no one could tell, James was looking forward to doing his very efficient work on his home turf.

When Forrest pulled out of Okolona on September twenty-second, only General Buford and his division accompanied him. Chalmers was left in Mississippi to do what he could to protect Meridian. Part of General Roddy's Alabama brigade met him in Florence, bringing his total strength to 4,000 troopers. The next day Forrest moved on to Athens, which by then had become a major supply depot for the Federals advancing through Georgia. There, showcasing his usual ingenuity, the General captured the entire garrison including 1,500 men, several hundred horses, an abundant supply of provisions, while ravaging several block houses and many miles of trestle which they guarded.

From Athens, the command turned north into Tennessee to begin the work of wrecking the Yankee communications that now stretched from Atlanta north through Chattanooga and Nashville onward to Louisville. After running into formidable infantry numbers around Pulaski, the General turned his columns east toward Fayetteville, where he again exacted considerable damage to many miles of valuable Yankee track. The Federals again came after their intimidating foe with vastly superior numbers. Before he lost a single trooper, Forrest had his entire command back across the Tennessee River and safely into Alabama.

By the middle of October, Forrest was contacted by Richmond with instructions to meet General Hood and The Army of Tennessee at Florence, Alabama, by November twenty. The grand old Confederate fighting machine of the West had been decimated by its recent struggles with the Federals under Bill Sherman. Hood had been selected to replace Joe Johnston because he would assume an offensive strategy where his defensive minded predecessor would not. Johnson realized the South risked loosing a large part of his force and, potentially surrendering Atlanta. With Atlanta's collapse, the last hope of a successful prosecution of the war fell as well. When Forrest's corps arrived at Florence on the eighteenth, Hood's gallant army was down to a mere 40,000 effective troops broken into three corps commanded by Cheatham, Stewart, and Lee, past commander of Forrest's department. With Hood was one division of cavalry under the command of Bill Jackson. Forrest was given overall command of the cavalry, bringing his total force available to some 8,000 riders.

Even after the recent debacles which the army had experienced, it was full of spirit as it marched toward the origin of its name. Unfortunately, the commander of this brave body of men was not the same man who had contributed so positively to the glorious achievements of The Army of Northern Virginia in its prime. John Hood, also known as Sam, though a willing and courageous fighter, was terribly maimed. He had lost the use of an arm on the second day at Gettysburg and had given a leg to the cause while leading a division of Longstreet's corps at Chickamauga. By November of 1864, Hood was riddled with both physiological and pyschological pain on a constant basis as a result of his wounds and the terrible beating he had taken in the battles for Atlanta. As a result, he had begun to use alcohol and laudanum on a daily basis in an effort to ease his pain. The damaged General was not the man to lead The Army of Tennessee on a last ditch effort to save the Confederacy in the West. Although the odds were extremely long, rational men such as Nathan Forrest gave the scheme a chance if properly executed and lead with vigor.

Although starting slowly, the campaign began well enough when Hood flanked Union General Schofield out of his fortifications at Pulaski on the twenty-third. By the next day, Schofield's army of 20,000 had retreated to Columbia and the South bank of the Duck River. It was here, between Columbia and Nashville, that Hood's plans began to fall apart in the last few days of November. With Schofield holding at Columbia, Hood conceived a plan to hold the Yankee force in check with one corps and his artillery while the other two corps circled to the East to gain the Union rear somewhere in the vicinity of the small rural community of Spring Hill. Realizing the strategic importance of the little hamlet to his rear and the vulnerable position of his force, Schofield dispatched a division of infantry to Spring Hill on the twenty ninth.

The division arrived in Spring Hill late in the afternoon about the same time as Forrest and his cavalry. As was usually the case, the efficient Forrest began his investment before the corps of Cheatham and Stewart arrived on the field. Expecting the added weight of the support of the infantry to help him close the door on the Federals, the General waited for Cheatham and Stewart to deploy their men for battle. With daylight running out, Forrest impatiently looked for the beginnings of an infantry advance to secure the desired discomfiture of the lone Yankee division. His cavalry, composed of many Tennesseans, fought ferociously expecting any minute to be reinforced by the infantry that was near at hand. The support never arrived.

While nearly exploding with adrenalin at the prospect of fighting in close proximity to his home, James was used extensively for dispatch purposes between the General and the Confederate high command. Twice he reported to Hood personally that Forrest had his troops positioned between the Union force at Spring Hill and Schofield at Columbia. On both occasions he was assured that orders had been given for the combined operations of the Confederate forces to assail Spring Hill. Even so, day turned to night and the infantry did not move. Forrest was highly agitated by the apparent mismanagement of the available forces. Letting opportunity slip away was not his game. With James in tow, he rode straight for Hood's headquarters for explanations. None were forthcoming. The two found their commander dull and under the influence. Forrest begged Hood to give him just one solid division of infantry with which he promised, "to bag the lot."

The General called on James, as a resident of the area who knew the lay of the land, to corroborate his view that the Federals at Spring Hill were ripe for plucking. Having served with a man of such stature as Nathan Bedford Forrest, James was not awed when he spoke to John Hood.

"General, sir, I grew up in Franklin, just a little north of here. I have traveled and hunted in this area many times since I was a child. I have seen the Yankee fortifications and know that there are many avenues available to us to get on either flank or even the rear of their force. I would be honored, sir, to serve as a guide in that effort."

Looking through glazed over eyes, Hood dismissed the pair with a slight wave of his hand.

"Orders," he slurred, "have been given to route that force. I presume they will be carried out by the corps commanders on the field."

"But, General," Forrest fumed, "they are not being carried out!"

Seeing that they were making no progress, the General stormed away to see to the needs of his own troops.

While Forrest had been pleading for assistance, Schofield had been informed of his precarious position. Assuming that his men at Spring Hill would be defeated and probably routed from the field by a vastly superior force, he had started the remainder of his forces north at twilight, again, assuming he would have to fight his way through to Nashville. What he did not anticipate was that Confederate bungling would allow him to march, almost completely unharried, within earshot of the Southern camps. Confederate troops encamped on either side of the Columbia/Spring Hill highway saw figures during the night marching northward within one hundred yards of their fires, and yet, no action was taken.

Amazed at the ease of his forced march, Schofield gathered his troops together at Spring Hill on the night of the twenty-ninth and proceeded on to Franklin. Once his consolidated force was safely beyond the resting Confederates, Schofield entrenched on the southern edge of Franklin with the Columbia highway running right down the middle of his line. He commandeered the Carter home as his headquarters and waited for the coming Rebel horde.

During the night, Forrest saw what was happening and could not believe his eyes. A golden opportunity was evaporating before him and he was powerless to stop it. While the rest of the army rested and waited for the dawn, he went to work. Jim and James were dispatched hard on the Federal's heels to ascertain their position as early as possible while the General began the process of putting his troopers in readiness for a potential flanking movement of the Yankee works.

As the Wilsons sat high atop Winstead Hill looking down on the Union army arrayed in front of them, the emotion of the sight overwhelmed them. Their stomachs were so tight, they could hardly speak. Each knew and understood what the other was feeling. Below, where once stood their fine home, all that was left was the foundation which had been built up with dirt to form Yankee entrenchments. The ground was covered everywhere by a creeping blue sea of motion as the Yankees prepared for the coming Confederate tide. Neither Wilson had prepared himself for a fight on his own soil. Active operations had not taken place this far north in their state since early in the war. To be coming home was one thing. Coming home to fight was quite another. As the sun was just beginning to turn night into day on that fateful November thirtieth, they settled in to gather themselves and wait for their comrades, who they knew were headed their way. At dawn, Jim Wilson spoke to his son for the first time since they arrived at their vantage point overlooking the valley that was their home.

"Are you alright, James? I've been so worried about you for several months now. I know that war does many things to a person, it certainly has to me. You've been so withdrawn from everything around us, I just haven't known what to say. I hope you know how much I love you, and, although I'm not in your shoes, I've tried to figure it out to help me understand.

"I know how much you miss Camille, cause I still miss your mother. I'm afraid that tomorrow's fight will be different from all the rest, at least for the two of us. I'm not saying these things to lecture you, believe me. I just don't want you to do anything rash and get yourself killed."

The passion swelling up within James was relentless. All of his pride slipped away as he sobbed and held his father. No one could ever replace the caring and love that he felt for this man, his parent and friend.

"So many times," he began, "I've wanted to talk, but was afraid, afraid of what would happen to me. I thought that if I let it out it might affect my judgement or interfere with my responsibilities. I thought it might make me less of a man. And, I've been so damn depressed that I just wanted to kill and kill some more. I haven't had any outlet other than the fighting.

"I know how ruthless I have been. There just didn't seem like there was any other road to travel. I guess it was wrong not confiding in you, but I couldn't find a way to talk. Being here with you changes all that. It seems it's all come down to this.

"Don't misunderstand, I'm not planning on giving it up. But, here we are, ready to fight a battle, on our own property. What scares me the most is that I want to live through this. And, I want you to be with me when its all over so we can go North together to find Camille and bring her back to whatever is left. But, as you said, this fight is different for us."

Early that morning when Hood awakened, he went into a rage because his instructions had not been followed. With Stephen Lee and all the army's artillery still on the south bank of the Duck River, he sent the corps of Ben Cheatham and A.P. Stewart chasing up the Columbia Pike after the Federals. In anticipation of just such a neurotic move, Forrest was actively probing the Union defenses in search of a route by which the Confederates could deliver a crushing blow. He thought he had found it on the Yankee right or western flank.

By eleven that morning, Hood had arrived and made his headquarters on the spot where the Wilsons had waited. Hood was flushed and furious, obviously already imbibing. As his renowned infantry began to file past taking up their positions for battle, he formulated his plans for a frontal assault on the Federal works immediately to his front. Both Cheatham and Stewart, along with several divisional commanders, including Pat Cleburne, protested strongly that such an attack with only two of three corps present with absolutely no artillery support, would be a disaster.

Again Forrest pleaded for just one division to be released to his command so that he could develop a flanking movement to the west past Carter's Creek. The commanding General interpreted the arguments of his subordinates as an unwillingness to fight in the open, reiterating his orders with emphasis. There was nothing left for those brave souls to do but to obey.

By one o'clock, the battle lines were arranged for the assault. Most of the divisional and brigade commanders prepared to go in with their troops for they knew that their only chance of success was for a terrific and courageous attack delivered with exemplary leadership. The cavalry was divided into two parts for either flank with Bill Jackson in charge of the left, while Forrest commanded on the right.

Shortly before the attack was scheduled to begin, the Wilsons arrived at the point where General Forrest was directing the placement of his troopers so as to hopefully gain the extreme Federal flank and rear. He had hoped the fight would be started before he saw them for he knew why they would come. At first, he tried to avoid their contact and succeeded due to the fact that he was extremely busy with details that only he could handle. But after several minutes, Jim Wilson stopped his old friend with an abrupt grab of the shoulder.

Angered and with a fierce look, the General turned and simply said, "What?"

Without saluting or showing any other sign of respect, the older Wilson replied, "I imagine you know why we're here. This is our home, Nathan, and we're not going to sit out on the flank and watch. We're going in with the infantry. Either with Pat Cleburne or General Adams."

"I'll be damned in hell if you are," bellowed their commander. "I don't care how you feel or what you think, I'm still in charge here. You're both staying right here with me. You're gonna have plenty of fighting to do with me. And believe it, we'll kill a mess of Yankees before this day is done. Now, damn it, get on your horses and be ready to move on my signal or I swear I'll shoot you both myself."

James began to speak, but his father cut him off, knowing that it was not his place to say to their General what he knew his son would say.

"You don't understand, General, we didn't come here to ask your permission. We came here to tell you what we are going to do and to ask you, if we don't come out of this one, to find us and take care of our remains.

"I tried to talk James out of going myself earlier today, but after a while, I began to see it. We just don't have a choice. Besides, if I go, he wants to go with me, and if he goes, I want to go with him. Now, we don't have much time, so please listen to what we've got to say."

No man had ever seen N.B. Forrest cry, and indeed, he didn't cry then but remorse was written all over his face as he sighed and acquiesced to listen to his most devoted followers.

James stepped forward extending his hand, "I respect you as much as any person I have ever known and serving under you was a pleasure. You have taught me more than anyone ever could. If I live through this, my experiences with you will have been invaluable to me. Also, there is the girl up in Maryland. You've heard of Camille Johnson. Let her know what happened and how. Coming from you, she will understand why we had to do what we did."

With a salute, James took one step backward. His father immediately took the hand of that giant among men and shook it solemnly but firmly.

"You know how I feel about you and what we've fought for all this time, so I won't repeat what's already been said. I hope I see you on the other side, but if I don't, I'll be looking forward to riding through hell with you."

He smiled and so did Forrest. With that, the two mounted their horses, turned and rode toward Winstead Hill.

Like Forrest, the Wilsons had known Pat Cleburne before the war. He gladly welcomed them to join his boys for the assault. In his finest ceremonial uniform of true Confederate grey, Cleburne looked absolutely resplendent. Smiling and ever confident of his troops, "The Stonewall of the West" said, "I'm certainly glad to have two such renowned fighters as yourselves to escort me to those entrenchments. I understand we'll be crossing right over your property. I want you right up front with me so we won't be misguided."

As his smile waned he said, loud enough for anyone close by to hear, "Boys, this will be short and desperate."

Just before the signal gun was fired, Jim Wilson took one more glance toward the east, as if he might see the General.

Then they were off. Fifteen thousand hard fighters of the Army of Tennessee, seven divisions strong in three neat rows stretching a full half mile, marching at route step with their weapons shouldered as if on parade. Within the hour one third would be down. But the others would keep on fighting.

Like that day at Antietam, James felt like he was going to vomit at any moment. But he knew he couldn't. He had to make sure his father was alright. Every few steps he looked to his left to make certain his father was keeping up. After all, there weren't many men in that charge that were over fifty years old. Every time he looked there was his father, looking back at him. They smiled, knowing one way or another, they were headed home.

About a half mile out, the Yankee artillery began to take a toll, knocking out several from the compact lines. James could hear the sergeants behind him bawling to "close up the ranks." Rabbits and squirrels scampered away from the oncoming tight formations. Within five hundred yards the Federal cannoneers changed from solid shot to canister, creating larger gaps in the lines. Stiil the Rebels pressed on.

Out of the corner of his eye James could see men falling, but others quickly filled the holes. At the four hundred yard mark,

James clearly saw the foundation stones of his home. Again, he looked to his father and there he was, grinning back.

"We're home, son," he shouted.

As if Pat Cleburne knew where the Wilson's had lived, just inside the boundaries of their land, he halted the men to dress the lines for the final push. Cleburne unsheathed his dress sword and held it high above his head as a signal to reform. Then many men were beginning to yell. Not the "rebel yell", but wild, independent screams more like a mob than an organized body of soldiers.

The fever pitch of battle was too much for many of them to control. Since their rifles were ineffective at that range, they let it out with their voices.

For a brief moment, Cleburne turned his back on the enemy to look back toward his troops in admiration. With a broad smile, he turned back toward the Union earthworks and lowered his sabre, the signal to close with the enemy. Instantaneously, the inspiring and frightening Confederate battle cry rolled off the lips of those vets of The Army of Tennessee as they broke into a dead run, everybody trying to beat everybody else to their objective.

As the dash began, James reached out to grab his father as they ran past their home. They could see the Yankees and hear the bullets as they whizzed by. The first line of Federals broke and ran for the cover of their second line some hundred yards behind the first. Yankees and Confederates were running side by side. The main Union line had to hold its fire so as not to hit their own men. The fleeing Yankees were stabbed and shot in the back as the commingled mass surged forward. Suddenly, they were among the Federals in plain view of the Carter house. Cleburne had his revolver in his left hand and his sword in his right, shooting and stabbing at everything blue. Jim Wilson had discarded his rifle for more accurate work with his two Colt revolvers. James was using his long blade to advantage. He saw Cleburne go down, riddled with bullets, but there was no time to stop. He and his father and several hundred others pounded through a break in the line right in front of Schofield's headquarters. The Yankees were running, success was at hand.

Once again, the rebel yell was heard above the roar of cannon and small arms fire, triumphant in victory. But it was not to be. Just as quickly as the break was achieved, it was plugged by reserves brought rushing from the rear. James turned to look for his father. As he did, he saw Jim Wilson take a minie ball in the chest and tumble forward. Just as quickly, he caught one in the back of his right leg. As he reached down to feel the wound, he was hit a second time, this time in his left thigh. As he fell to the ground, he could see many of his comrades raising their hands to surrender. The attack had failed, but the grey columns had proved their merit.

The McGavock home, Carnton, had been spared the ravaging years of war and the battle just completed only to bear witness to the slaughter and gallantry of the Confederate soldier, even in a vain effort. Late in the night of that fateful November thirtieth, the Federals pulled out of Franklin, leaving their own and Confederate wounded to the mercy of the town's inhabitants. The McGavocks opened up their home to serve as a hospital for the many wounded and dying soldiers.

When the Wilsons did not report back to him after the fighting ended, Forrest searched them out. He found them both, within a few feet of each other, and barely alive. He removed them from the carnage and took them to Carnton where the surgeons worked through the night and into the next day, trying as best they could to save as many as possible. He couldn't wait to find out if either would live or not. There was still a great deal of war left for him to fight. For his friends, he knew live or die, the war was over. For some 6,000 others, also, the fighting was through.

James regained consciousness on the morning of December second to the sounds of the moans of the many wounded who were housed at Carnton. He recalled having seen Cleburne killed in the terrible battle. Other Generals, Granbury, Gist, Adams, and Strahl had also been killed in the onslaught. All five were laid out on the front porch of the McGavocks mansion. General J.C. Carter had been mortally wounded and would not live long.

James, having lost a tremendous amount of blood and being

consequently very weak, could move but little. After realizing he was alive, his next thought was of his father, who he presumed to be dead. Only moments after opening his eyes, a hand touched his shoulder. It was his father who was propped up right next to him. Like his son, when Jim Wilson was brought into the shelter of Carnton and revived, he immediately sought his own blood. After the surgeons had dug the bullet out of his chest they had put him on a cot right next to James to wait for him to come to or die. When James first looked up and saw his father, he saw that same smile he had seen when they had started to run toward the Yankee works.

As Jim Wilson looked down at his son, he touched his lips with his finger, indicating for James not to talk. He said, frankly, "I knew we would make it and we did. Now we're through fighting. The war is probably close to the end. Our army is cut to pieces. There's not much fight left in anybody now, although, I'm sure what's left of our gallant army will try.

"It's only a matter of time. Once we're back on our feet, we have to start the rebuilding process, and that will be much harder than combat. The real test is yet to come. Are you up for it?"

Smiling back, James answered simply, "I'll try."

Afterword

General Forrest had much more fighting to do. In the last five months of the war, he, personally, was instrumental in saving the remains of The Army of Tennessee from almost certain destruction. At Nashville in late December, his rear guard action allowed the army the time to escape south to Alabama before being relocated to the Carolinas to contest Sherman's march north. The General and his small command of cavalry remained active until early May 1865, when he realized that continued fighting was useless in light of the capitulation of all other Confederate forces in the field. He remained a leader of stature in the South until the time of his death in October of 1877.

Both James and Jim Wilson recovered from their wounds, but not until after the end of the fighting in the spring of the next year. By June, James had made his way to Maryland where he married Camille with her father serving as best man. After the wedding, the couple moved back to Franklin where they began to rebuild the Wilson home and soon populated it with seven children, two of whom were named for the beloved General who had led their father through the last terrible years of war. Jim Wilson lived with his son, daughter-in-law, and grandchildren until his death in the summer of 1880.

Bedford Forrest visited the Wilson home often in the years following the war and relished telling the children stories of their father and grandfather and the late struggle for independence.